Praise for Pete J⸺
the **Louis the La**⸺

'In Louis, Pete Johnson⸺
boy who makes you laugh out loud.'
*Sunday Times*

'Pete Johnson is a wonderful storyteller.'
*Evening Standard*

'Fast, funny, and very readable.'
*Carousel*

'A rip-roaringly hilarious adventure.'
*The Book Trust*

'Funny and light ... the humour disguises
real emotional truth and depth.'
*The Guardian*

'A great story for boys and girls alike.'
*The School Librarian*

'This is such a brilliant book!'
'My daughter LOVED this book.'
'JUST BUY IT. YOU WILL NOT REGRET IT.'
'The best book I've ever read.'

# How to Change Your Parents into Superstars

Pete Johnson

OMMMMM!

HA HA!

AWARD PUBLICATIONS LIMITED

ISBN 978-1-78270-396-9

Text copyright © 2020 Pete Johnson
Illustrations by James Cottell, Nikalas Catlow and Angela Hewitt
This edition copyright © Award Publications Limited

First published by Award Publications Limited 2020

Published by Award Publications Limited,
The Old Riding School, Welbeck,
Worksop, S80 3LR

www.awardpublications.co.uk

20 1

Printed in the United Kingdom

*To the peerless Jayne and Claire,*
*of the Sheffield School Library Service,*
*with love and huge thanks for all your*
*support and encouragement.*

# A Favour

I've been kidnapped by the grumpiest man in the universe.

He held me prisoner in a large cupboard full of hideous plastic chairs. I had to stay there until my mum and dad rolled up.

So when I got home, what do you think was the first thing my parents did? Bake me a cake? Give me extra pocket money to make up for all the stress I'd been through?

NO. THEY SENT ME TO MY ROOM!

'You do realise the police were nearly involved today,' Dad wailed, shaking with anger.

'But, Dad, I was the one who was locked away in a cupboard...' I pointed out, not unreasonably.

'Louis... just go to your room!' he cried, in total exasperation.

7

'But I haven't told you what happened,' I began. 'It was something totally amazing.'

'We know exactly what went on,' sighed Mum wearily.

But they don't.

No one does – except Maddy. And me.

And I'm bursting to tell someone. So will you do me a favour? Let me fill you in on my incredible afternoon.

You will? Brilliant!

Shall we race on to the next page?

## Chapter One
# Slow-acting Magic

**Tuesday April 22nd**

**5.30 p.m.**
I'm Louis. Full name: Louis the Laugh. Pronounced Lou-ee, not Lewis like my old head teacher used to say all the time. I never corrected him though: he was a scary man.

I've only one talent – making people laugh. And I've dreamed of being a comedian since I was an amoeba.

Right now, I'm at school of course – yawn – but on Sunday afternoons I've been appearing on a vlog. You'll never guess which one! Prepare to be impressed.

Noah and Lily's vlog.

They're huge, aren't they? I mean, over three million teenagers have watched them cleaning their teeth.

Well, I've been featured on the end of some of their vlogs. You might even have seen me. I'm the cheeky-looking boy, with a head shaped like an onion, who helps kids with their problems and tells jokes.

Recently Noah and Lily even let me join in on one of their pranks. I was slapped across the face with a wet fish. I can't tell you how proud I felt. Shortly afterwards they Skyped me...

'You're so funny, Louis, and we really, really like you,' said Lily.

I beamed and quipped, 'I can understand that.' (I'm one of those people who has to make a joke about everything.)

'So we're going to miss you so much,' said Noah.

I stopped beaming. Miss me? But I wasn't going anywhere.

Only they were.

They were leaving to do a whole series of special interviews and pranks across America.

'I've got a passport,' I laughed (hint, hint). Noah and Lily chortled merrily. 'And a good friend of mine – Poppy, who's an ace conjurer –

is in America right now with her grandad doing some shows. I'm sure I could stay with them. So you needn't worry about my accommodation or my meals, or my washing...'

Noah and Lily laughed and laughed, then said they really had to go. I didn't understand why they weren't taking me seriously! Surely, they realised their ratings would plummet without me!

'Well, it's a brilliant opportunity for you both,' I croaked. 'How long will you be away?'

They didn't know. Months and months, anyway. 'Keep watching our show, won't you?' said Noah, just before they vanished out of my life.

Afterwards I sat there for ages in a kind of shocked daze.

Finally I told Maddy, my agent – and girlfriend, what had happened. She was stunned too, but then she said, 'Louis, I'll never forget the way you looked when Noah and Lily slapped that wet fish into your face. You were hilarious. And I'm so not letting a talent like that go to waste, no matter what Noah and Lily do.'

Two days later, Maddy found out about *Make Me Laugh*. A new talent show for young comedians. The producer, Marcus Capel, was doing auditions all over the country ('I could be in your town next week!'). But he also invited kids to send in three-minute audition tapes to give him a 'flavour of your personality'.

Maddy and I spent a whole weekend capturing 'my flavour' and then we waited eagerly for Marcus Capel's reply. One massive week crashed by. Then another...

NOTHING. There was, of course, only one explanation. My tape must have gotten lost in the post. So Maddy and I made another one and sent this off, by recorded delivery (ingenious or what?).

Here I'm going to briefly interrupt my story to let you in on a secret, which no one – not even Maddy – knows about. I was so desperate for Marcus Capel to reply, I made a wish.

I wished very quietly, 'If there's any magic out there in the world, let me hear from Marcus Capel.'

I don't actually believe in magic but there were so many books about wizards and all that carry-on, I figured it was worth a go, just in case. Anyway, absolutely nothing happened.

UNTIL THIS AFTERNOON!

It was the last day of the Easter holidays and Maddy and I had been to London where we'd met up with her two older sisters, Vicky and Zoe.

We'd had a day wandering round and watching the street performers in Covent Garden before they'd taken us out for a truly epic meal. We'd caught the train back and were slowly trudging out of the station – both of us had eaten far too much – when a loud, confident voice said to us, 'Excuse me, folks!' A guy with a hipster beard and wearing an open-necked white shirt and a velvet jacket bounced past us. A woman and a boy, about my brother Elliot's age (seven), trailed after him – lugging two hefty suitcases.

'What do you bet that man's an actor?' said Maddy.

'He even looks a bit familiar,' I said.

We watched him stride purposefully over to a dead posh car parked next to the taxis.

'I believe you are expecting me,' he said.

'That's class,' I murmured to Maddy, 'having a car waiting just for you.'

Then his name swept across the station like a tsunami: 'I'm Marcus Capel.'

That was so incredible it felt like, well... magic. Slow-acting magic – I'd put my request in weeks ago.

But just think, if Maddy and I had caught an earlier or later train, we would have missed Marcus Capel! Instead, our timing was magically perfect.

'He must be doing auditions,' I spluttered. 'We've got to find out where.'

Maddy didn't answer. She just stood there with her mouth slightly open, looking exactly as if someone had cast a spell over her. Then, all at once, she shook herself out of her stupor and said, 'We mustn't lose him.'

The next thing I knew, Maddy was charging after Marcus Capel. For a crazy moment I actually thought she was going to dive into his car with him. But instead she jumped into the back of the taxi, yelling, 'FOLLOW THAT CAR!' I hurtled after her. The driver twisted his head round and stared at us curiously. 'I've always wanted to say that,' she grinned.

As we took off, I asked, 'Maddy, what exactly are we doing?'

'Following Marcus Capel, of course,' she said, before adding, 'What do you bet he's going to a hotel? Probably the Belle Vue, that's the poshest hotel around here.'

'So, then what do we do?' I persisted.

Maddy was indignant. 'How do I know? I can't think of everything at once, can I?'

14

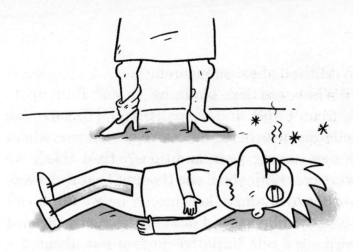

## Chapter Two

# The Hotel Comedian

We'd hardly got settled in the back of the taxi when, as Maddy had predicted, the Capel car pulled into the imposing drive of the Belle Vue. We asked the taxi driver to stop on the other side of the street, so we wouldn't be seen, and paid the driver as we watched the Capels stroll into the hotel.

'Now what?' I asked.

'Stop asking me that,' said Maddy. 'Just let me think for a minute.' She furrowed her brow with concentration and then said, 'Louis, you wait here.'

'Wait, what? Where are you going?'

'Popping inside the Belle Vue. I won't be long.'

With that, she disappeared.

What was she planning to do? Run up to Marcus Capel and casually say, 'Hi, sorry we followed you here, but can you tell me where you're having your auditions?' He'd think we were crazy! Maybe if she thought that if she was on her own and asked nicely, he wouldn't call security. Maybe he'd actually be really pleased we'd used our initiative to find out about the audition and he'd like us even more.

Maddy returned, smiling.

'So where are the auditions?' I asked eagerly.

'Haven't a clue. But Marcus Capel's room is number 41. You'll remember that, won't you?'

'Why, do I need to?'

'Yes. Because while I was in the Belle Vue, I had a brilliant idea.'

'Any chance of you sharing it with me?'

Maddy smiled triumphantly. 'You, Louis, are going to drop in on Marcus Capel.'

'Course I am,' I snorted.

'No, listen. I've got it all worked out. You'll go up to room 41 – take the lift.'

'You are too kind,' I murmured.

'Then you knock on the door and say, 'Welcome to the Belle Vue.' You'll pretend you work for the hotel, you see.'

'And he's really going to believe that, is he?' I

asked, incredulous.

'Yes, because you say you're the hotel comedian.'

'I've got a better idea. How about I put a sheet over my head and say, 'Hi, I'm the hotel ghost.''

'Louis, I'm serious,' said Maddy. 'After you've said, "Hi, I'm the hotel comedian," you go straight into your act. The one you sent him. The one I bet he's never seen. Well, this way, he'll have no choice but to watch it!'

'He can still chuck me out,' I said at once.

'He'll be too busy laughing. Also, he'll be thinking "What fantastic service. Not only do I get food and drink delivered to my door, but a top comedian as well." What's not to like?'

I hesitated. 'You make it sound so easy, but I bet—'

'Louis, this is probably the closest we'll ever get to Marcus Capel.'

'I do know that.'

'And we may never, ever get another chance like this – not in the whole of our lives.'

'I know that too,' I murmured.

'And once you get into Marcus Capel's room I am absolutely certain he will love you... and see your undiscovered comedy potential.'

Maddy had such confidence in me that it was like an extra bit of magic. The extra bit of magic

I needed to get me through the hotel door.

I looked at her for a moment. 'You know what?'

'What?'

'I think we can do this.'

'Yes! C'mon, we haven't got a moment to lose,' Maddy beamed.

'But he's only just got here.'

'He's a top executive so he is busy, busy, busy. Now listen, there's a receptionist and a security man, but I'll help you get past them.'

'How?' I asked.

'By fainting,' she whispered.

That was clever.

'It's not hard to look ill,' Maddy said as she started messing up her hair. 'I always manage to fool my mum. It just takes a few decent coughs to really "sell" it.'

'I never knew that.'

'I don't like to boast. So, the plan is, I'll shuffle up to reception coughing away, then say that I'm about to faint, and while I'm distracting everyone...'

'I shoot up to room 41.'

'Exactly,' she whispered triumphantly.

'Maddy,' I said, 'you really are the most brilliant agent in the world.'

She didn't argue with me. Instead she showed

me where, just inside the doorway, I could watch her, unseen.

'Remember,' she hissed, 'when I say, *I'm very sorry but I'm about to faint...*'

'I swing into action. Good luck, Maddy.'

'Good luck, Louis.'

And with that, she was off, stumbling and coughing towards the reception desk.

The inside of the Belle Vue was very large and very, very grand. There were chandeliers everywhere and loads of dead comfortable-looking chairs, but it was surprisingly empty.

A woman with green hair was squawking away like a parrot to a girl at the reception desk. 'Oh, I know you'll look after me very well. You always do.' Three teenage boys, all in expensive-looking sports clothes sprawled impatiently beside her.

Then, laden with bags and tennis rackets, they made their way towards the lift like a small invading army. A blonde giant in a red uniform lumbered forward and smiled sycophantically at the green-haired woman. She asked him how he was. But before he could reply, she was telling him all about herself – in great detail.

Suddenly, Maddy – who'd now reached reception – let out such a magnificent cough that even the green-haired woman briefly stopped babbling. Then Maddy announced in a wavering, breathless voice, 'I'm very sorry, but I think I'm about to faint,' and she started swaying about so convincingly that the girl immediately jumped out from behind the reception desk, and the giant security man sprang into action too.

Soon they were both helping a now wildly shaking Maddy onto one of the luxurious chairs. For a moment, I was just lost in admiration of Maddy's performance – she really was a class act.

But now it was my turn to move.

It was important to look carefree. So I put my hands in my pockets, then started to whistle, before breaking into a brisk walk.

The lift was right in front of me.

I never reached it. Instead, I went shooting right across the highly polished floor. I wasn't sure what had happened at first – I just found myself surrounded by legs.

'Well, help the poor boy up,' squawked the woman with the green hair, as six hands hauled me to my feet.

'I'm always telling them not to leave any of their bags lying about,' said the woman. 'That could have been a very nasty accident. Are you all right, my dear?'

'Never better,' I said swiftly. I was keen to be

on my way.

'Now, what's your room number?' she asked.

I hesitated.

'You must be in shock! You poor dear!' she cried. 'You've completely forgotten, haven't you?'

'Oh, but I've remembered now,' I said. 'It's 41.'

'Oh good, you're on the same floor as us. Come on, we'll help you.'

I darted a glance over at Maddy. She was now gulping down a glass of water as if she'd just been lost in the desert for a year – and keeping the security man and receptionist fully occupied.

Seeing she had everything under control, I allowed myself to be swept up into the lift by the family. And it was lucky I did, as you needed to have a room card to activate the lift.

'Now, would you like us to help you to your room?' asked the woman. I assured her I wouldn't. But then she called after me, 'You're going the wrong way for room 41. It's down that way,' she said, pointing me in the correct direction. 'Are you still a little bit confused, dear?' she continued.

'Maybe a bit,' I agreed. As I left, she began, rather loudly, to tell off her sons again.

Before I knew it, there it was.

Room 41.

No wonder my heart was pumping like crazy

and I was sweating buckets.

I knocked on the door and immediately a voice – Marcus Capel's voice – hollered, 'Come in.'

So that's exactly what I did.

BEST JOKES EVER!!

## Chapter Three
# Louis the Life-saver

I found myself in a vast room – in fact it was almost as big as our ENTIRE house – stuffed full of beds, chairs and tables. Mr and Mrs Capel were stood in front of a load of cakes with a confused-looking waitress. Not what I had been expecting.

Finally, the waitress, who had a long fringe and a bright white smile, said, 'I think you must be in the wrong room. Are you looking for your parents?' She was speaking to me as if I were a particularly dense two-year-old. I hadn't expected her to be here at all, let alone asking me questions, so that confused me for a start. I didn't like the way her eyes seemed to be drilling into me either.

So when I opened my mouth, not a word came out. I knew I was supposed to say something to Marcus Capel, about why I was popping into his room, but I'd completely forgotten what it was.

'Are you lost?' the waitress cooed again... She'd be asking me if I wanted my nappy changed next.

I swallowed hard. My mouth felt very dry. And I only knew one thing for certain: I couldn't start spouting any jokes. I wasn't at all sure if I could even speak. I was, in fact, a total let-down. Maddy was going to be so disappointed with me – and after all her superb coughing and shaking as well.

'No, I'm in the right room,' I managed to squeak at last. But, somehow, my voice was coming out as this high quavery sound, which I didn't even recognise as mine. 'I'm the...' But I still couldn't remember what Maddy said to call myself. 'I'm the...'

At that moment, I spotted the third Capel. He was right at the other end of the room, slouched over a plate of cakes. But he wasn't eating. Instead, he was choking silently and extremely vigorously, while his face turned a very deep red indeed. No one else had seen him.

'Don't worry,' I announced. 'I know exactly

what to do.'

In two bounds I was across that large room and crouching down beside the Capels' son. His parents, suddenly alerted to the fact their son wasn't currently in peak physical condition, clustered anxiously around me.

'What's his name?' I asked.

'Mason,' chorused his parents.

'Top name,' I said. 'Now, Mason, I want you to lean forward. That's it. What a great little mover you are.' I now had one arm around his tummy while I used my other arm to give him some short, sharp blows between his shoulder blades. And after the fourth blow, a tiny piece of cake shot out of his mouth and right across the room. 'Look at that go,' I said. 'Well done, Mason.'

His mum rushed forward with a glass of water.

'Not just yet,' I said, as Mason was still struggling for breath. 'Now you just need to relax. And I'll help you do exactly that, Mason. How do ghosts like their eggs? *Terror-fried.*'

His head started to shake.

'What do you say when King Kong graduates from university? *Kong-ratulations.*'

Then his shoulders started to judder.

'My dog chases everyone he sees on a bike.

What should I do? *Take his bike away.*'

It was the third joke that did it. Right afterwards Mason's mouth burst open as he laughed and panted – both all at once.

I let his mum and dad take over while the waitress, who'd been watching all this goggle-eyed, asked, 'How did you know what to do?'

'I am, in fact, the world's youngest doctor. Passed all my medical exams when I was only three years old... No, not really. I did this course at school.'

'You saved my life,' Mason said between gulps of air.

'Probably,' I said. 'But I don't like to brag.'

The next thing I knew, Marcus Capel was vigorously shaking my hand. 'We are very glad you came by, but I'm afraid I still don't know who you are.'

Now I remembered exactly who I was.

'I'm Louis the Laugh. And I'm here to welcome you to the Belle Vue hotel as I'm the hotel comedian.'

The waitress immediately shied like a startled horse.

'You probably don't know about me, I'm very new,' I explained, and well, that was sort of true, wasn't it?

'No,' the waitress agreed, her smile flickering

on and off like a worn-out torch now.

I turned to the Capels. 'In fact, you're my very first audience at the Belle Vue. So I want you all to relax and make yourselves comfortable while I entertain you.'

'What? Now?' asked Marcus Capel.

'Will it take long?' added his wife. 'I think Mason should really go and see a doct—'

But then Mason cried happily, 'Oh, brilliant!'

Marcus Capel, glancing fondly at his son's enthusiastic face, grinned and declared, 'Well, OK, Louis the Laugh, I suppose it's over to you.'

So I really was going to tell jokes to the producer of *Make Me Laugh*. Magic.

It had to be.

The three Capels settled together on one of the beds. 'It's all right, I'll take over now,' I said to the waitress. 'Have a good day, won't you?' She didn't take the hint though and lingered like a bad smell by the door.

'I'd like to start with one of my very favourite jokes,' I said. 'Two flies are playing football in a saucer. One says to the other, "You must practise." The other says, "Why?" "*Because next week we are in the Cup.*"'

Well, Mason laughed and laughed at that, making me even more pleased I'd saved his life. His parents were grinning too. And the waitress had slipped off somewhere. Perfect!

Very soon that room was rocking with laughter. I told all the jokes from my audition tape, and many others too. You see they were such a brilliant audience, I didn't want to stop.

Especially when I saw Marcus Capel wipe his eyes because he'd been laughing at me so much! Let me tell you that again, dear old diary, just in case you missed the sheer amazingness of that sentence.

*I saw Marcus Capel wipe his eyes because he'd been laughing at me so much.*

I'd almost finished when the waitress returned, but this time she was accompanied by that hulking security geezer and a little mousey-looking man in a purple suit, who had a small moustache, a long neck and a very haughty attitude.

'I must ask you to leave immediately,' Purple Suit said in a clipped steely voice. But I pretended not to hear him. I had two more jokes left – two of my very best (always end on a high) – and was absolutely determined to tell them.

So then the security man lumbered forward as if he was going to pick me up and waggle me about in the air a bit, just for good measure.

But instead Marcus Capel piped up, 'We'd so like to hear the rest of this young man's performance, which we are enjoying very much.' He said this with the same easy confidence that had first made Maddy and me notice him. With that, Purple Suit gave a very small nod to the security man who ambled back to him like a dog obeying its owner.

My last two jokes went down a storm. All three of the Capels clapped. Mason even jumped up and high-fived me.

Then I noticed Mason whispering something to his dad and Marcus Capel asked me, 'Louis, how would you like to perform at Mason's birthday party this June?'

'I'd like to very much,' I replied, giddy with delight.

'Well, here's my card,' said Marcus Capel. But before I could do anything a figure swooped in and seized the card.

Maddy.

'I've been listening outside the door,' she explained to Marcus Capel. 'I didn't want to distract my client. But I'm Louis's agent and deal with all his bookings.'

She had more to say too, but that's when Purple Suit very rudely barged right in front of Maddy and me. 'I am the hotel manager,' he announced, puffing out his chest and tapping his silk tie. 'These children have absolutely no business disturbing you – I can only apologise profusely for this intrusion.' Then he said to Maddy and me in a low, very menacing voice, 'You two, vacate this room at once!'

I didn't care for his tone at all. Hadn't he heard all that laughter? But I didn't want to be carried out by that security man either, so I gave Marcus Capel a very suave bow, and exited with Maddy.

Mason called after me, 'You should be on the telly!' I was liking that boy more and more. Marcus Capel didn't say anything, but at the door he did give me a light, friendly pat on the shoulder.

And then... Hang on, got to stop – footsteps are coming up the stairs.

## Chapter Four
# A Shocking Discovery

**6.25 p.m.**
The footsteps were Mum and Dad with my food rations. I've seen more cheerful firing squads. They stood sighing and shaking their heads at me for an excruciatingly long time.

'What you did today, Louis,' said Mum, 'was the stupidest thing you've ever done.'

I was going to start reeling off all the other, much more stupid things I've done in my life but thought better of it and instead said, 'I was discovered by a top TV producer!'

But instead of looking as proud and amazed as I was, they just shook their heads and sighed. They didn't believe me! 'What you do affects us

31

too, Louis,' said Dad, finally. 'We need to talk about this more but we are not going to give up our evening class. Our mindfulness course may even help us to de-stress.'

'When Marcus Capel puts me on telly, you'll de-stress all right,' I said.

Mum and Dad's eyes clouded over. Then Dad said in an *I'm really trying so hard to control myself* voice, 'Elliot will go round to Mrs Evans's house as usual and she's agreed to look in on you before we get back.' Mrs Evans is a neighbour whose son, Lee, is the best friend of my moronic brother. She's a real stick in the mud.

'Totally not necessary,' I began.

'You are not to leave the house OR have any visitors,' said Mum with a hard look. 'And as soon as we get back we will talk to you properly about today – and decide on a suitable punishment.'

'I've got goose bumps already,' I muttered darkly.

So off they went... anyway, let's forget them for now and return to the Belle Vue hotel. Where did I get to? Oh yeah, Maddy and I had just been marched off to the manager's office, hadn't we? Well, he ranted on about our appalling behaviour, but we put on our politest expressions, as all we wanted was to make a very swift exit. But then he said if we didn't give him our parents' phone numbers, he would call the police.

'How about if, instead, I come back tomorrow and put on a show free for all your guests.' I grinned hopefully. 'Two performances, if you like?'

The manager's moustache bristled furiously and Maddy whispered to me to give up on that one.

So, very reluctantly, we gave him our parents' phone numbers. Then the manager insisted Maddy and I were separated – yes, really. So Maddy went off with the waitress. But just before she was hauled out of there, she whispered, 'None of this matters. You've been discovered!'

Next, the security man deposited me in that cupboard, which I described to you earlier. 'Don't think much of my accommodation,' I said to him. 'Now, I'd like a plate of biscuits and a drink, please. The manager's paying.'

He scowled down at me from his not-inconsiderable height.

'The service in this hotel is terrible,' I called after him. 'I shan't ever stay here again.' After he'd gone, I discovered my phone had died on me. So there I was, trapped, with an army of plastic chairs and cut off from all civilisation. I bet this is what medieval torture must have been like. But when my parents FINALLY rescued

33

me, they didn't display a glimmer of sympathy –
and, well, you know the rest.

Still, Maddy's right, none of that annoying
stuff matters. Marcus Capel inviting me to his
kid's party is only the start, isn't it? This is only
the start of a beautiful new working relationship!

And when my boring relics find out I've been
telling the truth the whole time, and they see
what a glittering future awaits me – well, good
luck staying mad then, Mum and Dad.

**6.45 p.m.**
Wouldn't it be great if Marcus Capel made
contact before my parents got home? He'll
probably call Maddy first, as she's my agent.

**6.58 p.m.**
The doorbell has just rung. What do you bet it's
Maddy – and she has news from Marcus Capel
already? More soon.

**7.10 p.m.**
It was Maddy and she had news from *Marcus
Capel*.

But first she asked me how I was.

'All the better for seeing you, my dear,' I
quipped.

Maddy gave me a rather odd smile, I thought,

34

before asking, 'Do you want the good news or the not-so-good news?'

'Good news, definitely.'

'Well, I've already had a little chat with Marcus Capel.'

'Excellent.'

'And Marcus Capel said his son doesn't laugh easily – but he loved you.' She added, 'I could hear Mason laughing as I was walking up the corridor at the hotel.'

'It was wicked you turning up when you did,' I said.

'Well, the security man was busy with you and the receptionist had people checking in – so I just dived into the lift with a very friendly family. I must have heard over half of your act. You were terrific.'

'Thanks. So what's the not-so-good news?'

'Marcus Capel sells fridges.'

'A busy man.'

'As well as freezers and many other electrical goods.'

'I'm amazed he has the time,' I began, and then stopped. Maddy's face looked so grave, it stopped me in my tracks.

'Sadly, the Marcus Capel we met isn't a top TV exec,' said Maddy softly.

'But. But. But he must be! Are you sure?'

Maddy nodded slowly.

I gaped at her.

'Well, how dare he mislead us? I mean he's got the same name as a TV executive and acts exactly like someone high up in the media. No wonder he's caused all this confusion.'

'I'm very sorry—' began Maddy.

'It's not your fault,' I interrupted. 'It's him – the massive phoney.'

'Well, he's a big fan of yours.'

'He's got excellent taste then, but even so, we've made all that effort for some guy who flogs fridges.'

'He does also own several companies,' said Maddy.

'I don't care,' I began. And then I felt something bubble up in my throat. I thought I was going to do the worst thing ever – and cry in front of my manager and girlfriend – but, as I opened my mouth, I started to laugh.

Well, sometimes it's all you can do, isn't it? And soon we were both laughing uncontrollably, helplessly, and so loudly we didn't hear Mrs Evans let herself in. She stared at us anxiously. 'Oh dear.'

'Why, what have you done?' I asked, which set Maddy laughing all over again.

'Your parents said you weren't to have any

visitors, Louis – now, I don't want to get you into any more trouble, love…'

'It's all right, I'll go,' said Maddy.

'What on earth were you up to this afternoon, Louis?' asked Mrs Evans.

'This afternoon,' I said, 'I made Marcus Capel and his family laugh. He wasn't the right Marcus Capel. But you can't have everything, can you?'

**7.22 p.m.**
But why couldn't Marcus Capel have been the right one?

**7.23 p.m.**
If he had, I'm sure I'd be back at the Belle Vue hotel now, sinking into one of those plush chairs while he said, 'Louis, you really must let me plan your future.'

And I'd reply, 'Sure, but do you really think that I'm ready to appear at the O2 Arena?'

**8.10 p.m.**
Mum and Dad are back and so is Elliot. He bounced into my bedroom in his pyjamas. 'If you get sent away to boarding school, can I have your room?'

'Get out.' I sniffed. 'Do you ever wash?'

'No, never,' he admitted cheerily. Then right

37

outside my door he shouted, 'I'd so hate to be you right now.'

'I'd so hate to be you any time,' I called after him.

**8.15 p.m.**
I've just been summoned. Wish me luck.

## Chapter Five
# Full of Mindlessness

**8.50 p.m.**
Downstairs my parents asked, 'Shall we talk in the garden?' Which was a surprise (the first of many).

It was quite dark by now and we assembled round the side of the shed, like a small band of spies. I nearly asked them for the secret password. Unfortunately this wasn't the moment for jokes, as they both looked very serious.

'We're not often ashamed of you,' said Mum. 'But today we were. You cannot go round breaking into people's hotel rooms. Do you promise you will never do that again?'

As I hadn't broken into anyone's hotel room

today, that was quite an easy promise to make.

Then Mum announced, 'We know exactly why you did it.'

'You believed this guest was someone famous,' said Dad.

'And he almost was – had exactly the same name and everything,' I began.

Mum looked at me. 'It all really started with Noah and Lily going to America, didn't it? You felt they'd abandoned you – and that your big chance for fame and stardom had gone with them.'

Well, I was a bit shocked. I'd hardly spoken to my parents about Noah and Lily, but they'd noticed all the same. Talk about sneaky!

'And you dreamed of your life being exactly like Noah and Lily's, didn't you?' Mum went on.

How did they suddenly know so much about me? There was only one explanation: these weren't my parents at all. They were dead clever (possibly cyborg) look-alikes.

'During the break at the mindfulness class, we discussed what you did today,' explained Dad.

'Oh, great,' I muttered.

'It was in total confidence with Steve, our tutor,' said Mum. 'And anyway, Steve thinks what you did today was a cry for help.'

Well, Steve was a total idiot. I did it for one reason and one reason only – to get discovered.

'He thinks you've lost your sense of self-worth and so you need our help – and shouldn't be punished at all.'

Hang on, what?

Quick as a flash, I said, 'Steve – he's good, isn't he? He knows about this stuff?'

'We think so,' chorused Mum and Dad.

Then Dad said softly, 'Don't worry, Louis, we'll help you find your self-worth.'

I hadn't the faintest idea what he was warbling on about. But here's the most important thing: I wasn't being punished.

**9.03 p.m.**
'You are so lucky!' exclaimed Maddy when I told her. She hadn't gotten off quite so lightly and was having her pocket money stopped and was grounded until further notice.

'I know,' I laughed.

'So what do you think your parents will do now?'

'Be especially nice, I presume – and probably spoil me a bit. So for instance, I won't have to travel all the way downstairs for my meals any more. They'll deliver them to my bedroom door instead. And afterwards I'll only have to leave the plates outside for them to be collected.'

Maddy began to laugh.

'Plus, I think Mum should make me a chocolate cake. Not every day – that would be greedy. Once a week will be fine. But eating a big slice of cake every night will do wonders for my self-worth. Actually, Maddy, I'm sort of looking forward to the next few days.'

## Wednesday April 23rd

**4.08 p.m.**
When I got home Mum and Dad were waiting for me in the kitchen.

'Good day at school?' asked Dad.

'A bit tiring.' I sighed heavily. 'Do you know what would so help me now? A slice of your chocolate cake, Mum. I know you're very busy, but if you could make one—'

'Louis,' Mum interrupted, 'how do you fancy a trip out on Saturday?'

'Why... are we going somewhere good?'

'We are,' Dad grinned.

'It's not Alton Towers, is it?' I asked eagerly. 'A day there would help my self-worth no end.'

'No,' said Dad, 'something even better.' He went on, his voice vibrating with enthusiasm, 'A special introduction to mindfulness for families.'

'What!' I spluttered.

'It was already oversubscribed,' said Mum, 'but after a bit of expert pleading from both of us' – she smiled over at Dad – 'they've very kindly sneaked us in.'

Dad's grin grew even wider. 'We said we'd help you, didn't we, Louis?'

'Er, did you say this Saturday?' I asked.

'Yes, but only from 9 a.m. until lunch time,' he replied.

ONLY. A shudder ran right through me. 'Sorry, but I can't make it. I've just remembered I'm very busy.'

'Doing what?' demanded Mum.

'Dunno yet... but give me a couple of minutes and I'll think of something.'

'Louis, son,' started Dad, 'being nervous is natural. Your mum and I were more than a bit apprehensive when we first joined the course.'

'We certainly were – especially me. In fact, I was positively suspicious,' said Mum. They had a bit of a chuckle about that; parents are weird. 'But you need to step outside your comfort zone to stop yourself getting locked into the same way of thinking. And this evening class has given us a whole new way of looking at life.'

'I'm happy for you,' I said, 'but you know how you two love going to garden centres and get all excited when you spot a lesser-spotted delphinium, while I'm bored out of my mind – well, it'll be the same with mindlessness.'

'You don't know that,' said Dad.

'And it's mindfulness not mindlessness,' Mum cut in. 'There'll be lots of other children there too.'

'All we're asking,' said Dad, 'is that you give it a chance.'

'Couldn't you just go and tell me about it afterwards?' I suggested.

'No, Louis, because there are follow-up activities too.'

'Follow-up activities?' I replied weakly. Then I asked, 'Is it too late for me to be adopted?'

They both laughed then.

They thought I was joking.

## 5.45 p.m.

So the TV was babbling away in the corner of the kitchen – my parents often have it on at this time and, as usual, it was tuned to *Live at Five*. Anyway, I'd just wandered into the kitchen – no one else was about – when I heard Clive, the leathery old host introducing this week's Internet Sensation – Noah and Lily.

And on they bounced. Only they both had Post-it Notes stuck all over their faces. Apparently, this was to remind them of all the things they had to do before they flew to America tomorrow. And then Clive talked about how Noah and Lily were always doing wacky challenges and how he had one for them now – to eat a tin of dog food live on air. While they were tucking in, Maddy called me.

'Are you watching—?'

'Yes,' I interrupted.

'I am so angry!' she cried. 'It should be you on television eating dog food – not them! And one day, it will be.'

I loved her confidence.

But right now that future day seems such a long way off.

## Chapter Six
# Selfie Time

**Thursday April 24th**

**4.40 p.m.**

On my way home from school, I noticed a girl on the other side of the road, smiling very shyly at me. She had a long, friendly face and sparkling dark eyes. 'I could be wrong,' she began as she came toward me, 'but aren't you Louis the Laugh?'

I grinned – a fan! 'You can call me Louis.'

'I'm Isla, and no one special at all. But I've watched you every week on Noah and Lily's vlog, and you are totally hilarious.'

'I only did a bit of chatting – nothing special,'

I replied with my usual bewitching modesty.

'Well, you always cheered me up and your smile is so infectious... but I've missed you lately. All the shows are just about Noah and Lily's trip to America. When are you coming back?'

'Not exactly sure.'

She looked shocked. 'But the show is nowhere near as good without you.'

'Well, I can tell you, Isla, the ratings have really gone down since I stopped appearing. And that's a fact. Well, a sort of a fact. All right, I just made it up.'

She laughed. 'I knew you lived nearby, but I never imagined I'd be talking to you like this. I so wish you went to my school.'

'What school is that?'

'Barnes. Do you know it?'

'Oh, that's dead posh.'

'Not really, and I'm not the least bit posh. Louis, I bet you get asked this all the time, but could I have a selfie with you? You can totally say no if it's a total pain!'

In the end, Isla took three selfies.

'My boyfriend will be so jealous when he sees this.'

'Will he?'

'Oh yeah, because you make him laugh too. In fact...' Her voice suddenly fell. 'Hang on... Did you know we're being watched?'

'Not by your boyfriend?'

'No, by a boy acting very strangely over there. He's staring at us while taking stuff out of the rubbish bin and then putting it straight back in again.'

I looked over to where Isla was pointing and saw... Edgar.

Edgar is Maddy's only other client. He writes poems that no one, not even Edgar, understands. He is 13 but acts as if he's 180.

'Edgar,' I called, 'what on earth are you doing?'

'Good afternoon,' he called back. 'Some people haven't been disposing of their crisp packets in the right way. And if you don't scrunch them up properly when the bin gets very full, like this one, they will fall out again, causing litter to fall on the ground—'

'Can I withdraw the question,' I interrupted, 'and ask you to come over here and meet Isla, who thinks you're incredibly weird, which you are.'

She giggled as Edgar sloped over. Edgar's got very neat blond hair, which always looks immaculate – just like everything else about him. In fact, clean, soapy smells positively ooze off him. I can't hold it against him though. Not really.

'I am pleased to make your acquaintance,' he said to Isla.

'Didn't you used to go to my school?' she asked.

It seemed he did. After telling Isla he now had lessons at home, Edgar suddenly began twisting his face about. I'm not certain, but I think he was trying to smile. But it was pretty terrifying. Unsurprisingly, Isla left shortly afterwards. There was a rather odd silence then.

'Edgar: The Litter Warrior,' I said at last.

He ignored this and instead said very slowly, 'I consider Maddy the very best person I know.'

'So do I... and as for Isla, if you're wondering – which I know you are – I've never met her before.'

He looked disbelieving. 'Yet I saw you having pictures taken together.'

'She's watched me on Noah and Lily's vlog and wanted to have a selfie.'

Edgar shook his head. 'You're telling me she wished to have her photograph taken with a complete stranger. And what on earth is she going to do with it?' He gave one of his rare laughs before leaning forward. 'So you won't be seeing her again?'

'No,' I said firmly.

'Then I shan't mention this incident to Maddy. Mum's the word.'

I was about to say there was no need to keep it secret when — and don't ask why — I decided against it and said, 'Cheers, Edgar.'

**Friday April 25th**

**5.42 p.m.**

'How am I going to survive it?' I asked Maddy and Edgar. We were round at Maddy's as she was still under house arrest. 'A whole morning of being mindless.'

'It's a severe punishment,' agreed Edgar. 'It appears your parents have been hoodwinked by all this mumbo jumbo.'

'And don't forget the threat of follow-ups,' I added.

'That's beyond horrible,' said Maddy.

'So how can I escape my truly horrible fate?' I asked. 'Come on, think of something fast.'

'You could just refuse to go,' said Maddy. 'I know, why don't you tie yourself to your bedpost as a protest.'

'That'll only make them more determined,' I said gloomily. 'You see, they're doing this for my own good.'

'Parents are at their most mad and unreasonable when they think that,' said Maddy.

'I believe,' said Edgar, 'you should use your

humour tomorrow to expose the ludicrousness of all this New Age nonsense.'

'Tell jokes, you mean?' I asked.

'Yes, as the one thing these New Age hippie types hate is being laughed at,' agreed Maddy. 'You might even get thrown out of the class!'

'That's a truly brilliant idea,' I said. 'I knew you wouldn't let me down.'

**8.00 p.m.**
Maddy's just rung. 'This will cheer you up,' she said excitedly.

And it did.

She's only got me another gig! It's for a new online show called *Dare to be Different*.

Maddy said they were dead keen to hear all about my dream of being a comedian. (Well, I can rattle on about that forever!) They even want to interview me next week and will travel to my house.

'I'm finally getting the star treatment,' I said.

'You so deserve it,' said Maddy.

One big problem, though. Or rather two: Mum and Dad.

I had to pick a time when all my family were away, so Mum and Dad couldn't sabotage the whole thing. Then I remembered Mum had told me she was taking Elliot to a birthday party after school on Tuesday and probably wouldn't be back until half-past five. Tuesday was also Dad's day for working in London, so he's never back before six o'clock.

After I'd explained this, Maddy said briskly, 'Right, I will tell them you have a window on Tuesday from four p.m. until half-past five.'

'It's such a shame about all the secrecy,' I said. 'It isn't as if I'm doing something bad. All I want to do is entertain the nation.'

'And you will,' said Maddy. 'This time nothing will go wrong.'

## Chapter Seven

# Banned from Telling Jokes

**Saturday April 26th**

**7.40 a.m.**

I was woken up by someone bouncing on my bed, screeching, 'I hate you!' When I opened my eyes it was no great surprise to see Elliot glaring down at me.

'Are you doing an impression of the most annoying seven-year-old in the world?' I asked him. 'Because, if you are, it's very good! Anyway, what's upset your tiny, mad brain?'

'Mum and Dad say I've got to go to this mind... mind...'

'Mind the gap?' I suggested.

53

'No! Shut up! Mindful-thingy. And it's not fair because I've got to go as well as you, and I haven't even done anything wrong.'

I sat up in bed. 'I'm going to make sure we never get invited to another one of these courses – ever. But I need your help.'

Elliot immediately stopped bouncing and asked eagerly, 'What are we going to do?'

So I told him the plan.


**8.40 a.m.**
So here I am, in the foyer of the leisure centre. All the relics are chatting away excitedly, while their kids stand beside them – long-suffering and miserable. I exchange sympathetic smiles with several of them.


**8.50 a.m.**
We pile into a large room, with a low sofa at the front and cushions scattered everywhere. A tape with someone playing the violin drones on and on and on in the background…

'I feel calmer already,' Mum said.

How in the name of sanity can being crammed into a room full of loons, while someone screeches away on a violin, make anyone feel calmer?

\*　　\*　　\*

**9.15 a.m.**

A smallish guy with a long grey ponytail bounded in at the front to the sound of audible gasps. No one could quite believe what he was wearing – orange jeans, blue boots, a skull and crossbones scarf and, worst of all, a truly hideous sparkly jacket which made him look like a human glitter ball.

'Does he normally dress like that?' I asked Mum.

'No,' she said, and even she sounded a bit shocked.

'I've got a headache just looking at him,' I murmured.

'So have I,' Elliot chipped in. 'In fact, I can hardly see at all.'

'For the sake of Elliot's eyesight I think we should all go home now,' I suggested.

'Be quiet, both of you,' snapped Mum.

'I'm Steve,' announced the human glitter ball, 'and it's wonderful to see so many new faces as well as lots of my regular, not-quite-so-young faces. Ha-ha, ha-ha. Now, I expect you're asking yourself what on earth has happened to Steve... Did he get dressed in the dark? Ha-ha, ha-ha.' He tittered at his own joke before continuing. This time his voice rose. 'I put these clothes on, all found at jumble sales, you might not be

55

surprised to learn – ha-ha, ha-ha – to remind myself that true happiness can only ever be found within. I'm also challenging society's obsession with superficial things, such as how we look.'

Unbelievably, he got a large round of applause for spouting that bilge and for looking as if he'd escaped from a particularly tacky pantomime.

**9.24 a.m.**
Steve brought on his 'best buddy' Marianne, who was also all glittery and gushy, and when she smiled – which she did 99% of the time – you could see every single one of her teeth. She seemed to have twice as many teeth as any other sane human too.

'Now I want you,' she cooed, 'to ask the person sitting next to you what's the first thing they noticed about this amazing room.'

I turned to Elliot, who sniffed hard and then announced, 'I think someone's peed in their pants.'

'Brilliant,' I replied. 'You're a natural at mindlessness.'

**9.50 a.m.**
Next Marianne said she was going to teach us how to breathe – as if this is something we'd never done before.

'First of all,' she announced, with one of her megawatt grins, 'to help you relax, it's vital you breathe from the diaphragm.'

My hand shot up. 'Excuse me, Marianne, I've left my diaphragm at home today.'

Elliot started to laugh. At the same time he let out this really loud fart, which came out with such force that the sound exploded through the room. Elliot was rolling about on the floor now, red-faced and shaking with laughter. 'I apologise, Marianne, for my little brother,' I began, 'and the smelliest fart the world has ever known.'

All of the younger half of the room were laughing away and holding their noses.

But Mum wasn't. Instead she snapped, 'Outside, both of you, now!' then said, 'I apologise, Marianne, Steve, for such immature behaviour from my boys.' The next thing I knew she and Dad were steering Elliot and me towards the door.

Wow, I thought, Maddy and Edgar are going to be incredibly impressed. It's not even ten o'clock and I've been chucked out already.

**10.05 a.m.**
Except I hadn't.

Instead, Elliot and I received a massive

telling-off from my parents in the foyer. And if they were mad at me at the Belle Vue, they were furious now. Absolutely furious.

'I blame you entirely for this, Louis,' said Mum. 'We know you encouraged Elliot to misbehave.'

'Yes, he made me do it,' agreed my ever-loyal brother. 'I didn't want to do it.'

'Remind me to annihilate you later,' I muttered to him.

'You never even gave this morning a chance,' said Mum. 'Don't you want to enhance your overall well-being and learn how living in the present moment will—'

'Look,' I interrupted. 'This mindlessness lark is just not for me. But there's nothing to stop you going back in there and having hours of fun with your diaphragm. And I'll wait here for you. I've got all the Jeeves short stories on my tablet so I'll chill out reading them.' I even sat down and got my tablet out. 'So forget about me and enjoy yourselves – just as I'm going to enjoy myself. Everyone's happy.'

'Louis, stand up right now,' ordered Dad. 'We are not going to let you throw away this chance.'

Then Mum, in a very steely voice, said, 'This is what you will do. There is break time soon.'

'Oh brilliant! I'll—' I began.

'Enough,' Dad cut me off. 'That's when you

and Elliot will go to Steve and Marianne and apologise for your very silly behaviour and ask if they will, very kindly, allow you to come back. And when you do go back,' Dad continued, 'you will not try to be funny.'

'Bit harsh,' I muttered.

'Or tell any silly jokes,' snapped Mum.

'Or try to be the centre of attention in any way,' said Dad.

'You don't want me to be myself, then,' I said half as a joke.

But Mum cried excitedly, 'That's it exactly. Instead, we want you to find the new you.'

'The real you,' said Dad.

But that mad joke-teller was the real me! Only this didn't seem the moment to point that out.

**1.05 p.m.**

When Steve finished, people clapped and clapped. It must be with relief, I thought, that it was FINALLY OVER.

Only then Steve cried, 'Now I really want to keep the energy flowing.' Oh no, I thought, he's not going to do an encore, is he? But instead he started plugging some 'drop-in' session he was running on Tuesday afternoon and I was actually relieved I would be at school and so couldn't be dragged along to that as well.

'One very last thing, my friends,' Steve said. 'You've seen me in my fun clothes, ha-ha, ha-ha. Next time we meet, why don't you turn up in some fun clothes too. In fact, that's my challenge to you.'

'Don't you dare,' I immediately whispered to my parents, as they were at a highly impressionable age.

'We will be like a secret society,' grinned Steve, 'reminding ourselves how utterly unimportant our appearance is and that what is *truly* valuable can only be found *within.*'

Still more applause, before people started getting up and I gave a huge yawn... I would never complain about double maths being boring again.

It was then I noticed Mum and Dad watching me. They didn't say a word, just exchanged highly disappointed glances. And for a moment, I felt horrible. And then I was furious. How dare Mum and Dad make me feel horrible when all this is their own fault, dragging me here when I had far more important things to do – like sleeping?

They really are unbelievably selfish.

\* \* \*

**4.00 p.m.**
Tap, tap, tap on my bedroom door and in trooped Mum and Dad. They plonked down on my bed. 'Is there anything you want to talk about?' asked Mum.

'Yes, what are you both doing in my bedroom?'

'We meant about this morning,' said Dad.

'We know you found it very challenging,' said Mum, 'and that's why you behaved as you did. We picked up this leaflet for you,' she added. 'It's written by Steve.'

'No, thanks. I'm sure there's nothing I need in there. Why did you even make me go today?'

'Very simple,' said Dad. 'Because we're your parents, and it's our job to help you—'

'Excuse me,' I interrupted, 'but your job is to help me by feeding me and cooking all my meals, giving me money, driving me places and, did I mention, give me money?'

They smiled faintly. 'Oh Louis, you don't always have to work against us. We're here for you.' Then Mum added, 'We're not giving up on you.'

'Your mum and I,' said Dad, 'are on a journey of self-discovery. And we are going to take you with us.'

'Whether I want to or not,' I added under my breath.

## Chapter Eight

## Bombshell

**Sunday April 27th**

**11.05 a.m.**
Maddy rang.

'Can you come round for a few minutes?'

'Let me check my social calendar... yeah, doing absolutely nothing, as usual.'

'Edgar is here and needs some advice – from you.'

'From me? That sounds sensationally unlikely.'

'I know,' agreed Maddy. 'But you are the only person he wishes to talk to. No one else!'

**11.58 a.m.**

Maddy opened the door to her sitting room and said, 'You guys get comfy, I'll be right back,' and promptly left us alone in stony silence.

Edgar was sitting on the edge of the couch. He cleared his throat. 'This is awkward,' he began.

'Would a biscuit help?' I asked. 'Because it would help me. I'm starving. Haven't eaten anything for a whole ten minutes.'

Edgar ignored this. 'When you introduced me to Isla that afternoon—'

'Why are we talking about her?' I interrupted crossly. 'I met her once. She's a fan and wanted a selfie… that's it.'

'I know that. I just wondered if during my conversation with Isla, my fun side came across at all – because I do have a fun side, you know.'

'I'll take your word for it.'

'My problem,' said Edgar, 'is that my preferred form of communication is paper. I believe I can be extremely lively, maybe even witty, on paper. Anyway, I've set myself a challenge – to converse with people my own age. I might even attend a party. So I thought – well, Maddy and I both thought – you would be the best person to give me some tips.' Edgar got up. 'So could we pretend we are meeting at a party, and you decide if my opening comments strike the appropriate note?'

'Erm... sure, go for it.'

So Edgar started walking towards me, but instead of just walking, he started to shake his head from side to side in these weird little buzzing movements.

'What on earth are you doing?' I asked.

'Well, I thought it might help me blend in if I seemed to be nodding along to the music.'

'But you're rolling your head about as if you've just had ten electric shocks. And if you walk in like that, someone will ring for an ambulance. You've got to nod gently and be more subtle, like this.' I started to demonstrate.

'Actually, I think I'll forget that part,' said Edgar. So instead he advanced on me with one of his truly terrifying smiles and said, 'Good evening, delighted to make your acquaintance. I trust you are in excellent health... How's that for a beginning...?' Before I could reply he said, 'It was terrible, wasn't it?' He sank down on the couch again, sighing heavily. 'Why do I find the prospect of any sort of conversation with my contemporaries so utterly perplexing?'

I plonked down beside him. You had to feel sorry for the poor guy. So I told him something I had never told anyone else, 'Years ago I discovered the world is divided into cool people – and people who look like me. But later I found out something else. No one, not even the super-cool ones, are very confident about themselves. Not really. We're all scared inside. So you might as well just be yourself. There is only ever going to be one Edgar – for which I am very grateful. So just enjoy being him and stop worrying about what impression you're making.'

He stared at me for a long moment. 'You're not quite as stupid as you look, are you?'

'Edgar, that's the nicest thing you've ever said to me.' We sat in silence for a minute before I said, 'One tip, though – maybe give people a little warning when you're going to smile at them.'

## Monday April 28th

**4.10 p.m.**

On my way home from school I met Isla again. I think she might even have been looking out for me.

'Hi, remember me?' she yelled, running to catch up with me.

'Yeah, course. Hi, Isla.'

'I sent off a text to Noah and Lily about you, yesterday. I said their show wasn't half as good without you.'

I was touched. 'Thanks very much.'

'It's only the truth. So, are you working on any other shows?'

'Actually, I am,' I said. 'Have you heard of *Dare to be Different*?'

'I don't think so.'

'Well, you will do. They're interviewing me tomorrow.'

She looked dead impressed at that. 'That's awesome! Will you be going to a studio?'

'No, they're coming over to my house.'

'Wow, they must be keen,' she said.

I grinned. 'So how are you?'

She looked away. 'Don't ask.'

'I just have.'

'Charlie, my boyfriend, has been seeing Tiffany, my so-called best friend, behind my back. And everyone seemed to know about it except me. And now I'm the one who got dumped even though they were the ones sneaking around.'

'He must be mad,' I blurted out. Why was I so jumpy all of a sudden?

'Of course, everyone's gossiping about it – but they suddenly stop talking about it when they see me, which makes it even worse ... So, Louis the Laugh, what would your advice be to me? Imagine I called in to Noah and Lily...' She was looking right at me now.

'I'd say, allow yourself to be gloomy and

angry and miserable for a couple of days, then get dressed up and make sure everyone – and especially Charlie and Tiffany – see you don't care any more. And you'll find a new boyfriend and a new best friend in no time at all.'

She smiled. 'I might even do that. By the way, Charlie was really jealous I got a selfie with you. I think he'd like one too. He's mad about famous people.'

'I never normally refuse a selfie with a fan,' I said, 'but in his case, I would. How about that?'

She grinned. 'I'm so glad I saw you today. You've really cheered me up – and good luck tomorrow with *Dare to be Different*. I can't wait to see it.' She smiled shyly. 'I really am your biggest fan.'

**5.20 p.m.**
A bombshell!

*Dare to be Different* have just sent Maddy the final details for tomorrow. All looked fine until we saw that, as I'm under 16, YOU MUST HAVE A GUARDIAN WITH YOU TO SIGN THE CONSENT FORM.

Maddy's voice trembled down the phone as she asked me, 'What can we do?'

'Say I'm an orphan,' I said at once.

'So who's looking after you?' asked Maddy.

'Good point. OK, my parents couldn't get back in time but they've left a note saying it's all fine – which we could forge, of course.'

'But what if *Dare to be Different* say they need a parent to be actually physically there?'

'OK... they're both scientists, investigating invisibility – only their latest experiment has gone horribly wrong, so although they are here, no one can actually see them.'

Maddy laughed. 'It's original, but I don't think they'll fall for it.'

Then I asked, 'Do you remember when you pretended to be my mum so I could get into that audition at—'

'How could I forget?' interrupted Maddy. 'And I was awful!'

'No, you weren't. You even had that great wig.'

'Which kept moving!'

'Only once or twice... have you still got it?'

'I could probably find it.'

'And your "mum" voice was excellent. You have a definite talent for sounding old. And I think you've improved at acting since then – I mean, that fainting spell at the Belle Vue was superb.'

'I was rather proud of my cough,' admitted Maddy shyly.

'So why don't you pretend to have a bad cold when you're being my mum. Then you only need to shuffle in, sign that form, natter a bit about the weather – adults always go on and on about the weather – and then let rip with one of your magnificent coughs before tottering off again. You won't need to do another thing.'

'OK. But I think I should do a few more coughs upstairs,' said Maddy, 'just to keep it authentic.'

'You're such a professional.'

'The only thing is,' Maddy said, 'all this week I'm supposed to come straight home from school.' Her voice rose defiantly. 'But, it's fine, I'll just tell them I'm in detention.'

'Now nothing can stop us,' I said.

## Chapter Nine

# My Other Mum

**Tuesday April 29th**

**6.15 a.m.**
I've been awake for hours already.

Today's the day I'm being interviewed by *Dare to be Different* – and I get to meet my other mum again.

So, if that's not a day to remember, I don't know what is.

**6.32 a.m.**
Just heard someone downstairs – and Mum and Dad never get up until seven o'clock.

So, who is it?

**6.33 a.m.**
Burglars? Not likely... is it?

**6.34 a.m.**
Next question – what am I going to do about it if it IS burglars? Tear downstairs and be incredibly brave?

**6.35 a.m.**
That's exactly what I'll do – only not right now.

**6.36 a.m.**
Right now, I'll just bury my head under the pillow and... hold up, I've just heard laughing. Now I'm sure it's Dad.

**6.37 a.m.**
I'm definitely investigating now.

**7.02 a.m.**
Downstairs, I discovered something that was beyond weird. Mum and Dad were sitting cross-legged on the kitchen floor and breathing so heavily it was as if their life depended on it.

'Aha,' said Dad when he spotted me.

'Aha, yourself. What on earth are you doing?'

'Mindfulness is a wonderful way to centre yourself before you start the day,' Dad smiled.

71

'I'll take your word for it,' I said.

'It also makes you notice so much more,' Dad grinned. 'Do you know what I'm noticing now?'

'Amaze me,' I muttered.

'I'm picking up,' said Dad, 'that you'd like to join us but are too shy to ask.'

Well, he'd 'centred' in on the wrong thing there, all right. But the next thing I knew, they'd made a space for me and I was sitting cross-legged between them.

'What we're doing,' explained Mum, 'is breathing in for four seconds, then holding our breath for another four seconds, and finally letting our breath out very slowly, while counting to eight.'

So I joined in with them, just to be one of the gang. But then I said, 'Well, I've had masses of fun, but I don't want to wear my diaphragm out. Cheerio.'

But Dad put a hand on my shoulder. 'Will you do something for me?'

'Provided it doesn't involve breathing,' I murmured.

'Pretend I'm not your dad and this isn't your mum. No, we're just a couple of mates... inviting you to come and relax with them.'

'Thanks, Dad, but—'

'You're forgetting your dad's not here,' he

interrupted. 'Look at me, I'm one of your... dudes. Is that what you call them?'

'Never,' I murmured.

'So come on,' urged Dad. 'Let us three dudes share a moment of deep relaxation together. Now, do you ever feel restless, Louis?'

'Feeling pretty restless right now, actually,' I began.

'And your thoughts are all over the place,' he continued. 'Well, here is a word – you might even call it a magic word – which will instantly calm your mind, and help you concentrate too. *Om.*'

'Om,' I said flatly. 'Sorry, absolutely nothing happened. And if Steve told you to say that, well, I'd ask him for my money back.'

Dad smiled. 'You breathe in and say the word very slowly like this... *OMMMMmmmmm.*'

'And when you do breathe out, let the sound vibrate inside you,' urged Mum, 'sending so many positive waves rippling all through your body.'

'We'll do it together a few times,' said Dad. 'And then we'll have a group hug.'

'So much to look forward to,' I whispered.

**7.08 a.m.**
I so wish it had been burglars downstairs. Well,

73

they wouldn't have made me say *Om* with them for ten whole minutes, would they?

**8.00 a.m.**
I needed to make completely sure Mum didn't come home early today. So I asked Elliot, 'Would you like to earn five pounds?'

He nodded cautiously.

'All you've got to do is stay at this party today until half-past five.'

'You'll give me five pounds for that?'

'I will,' I said.

'What are you up to?' asked Elliot.

'Nothing for you to worry about.'

'Oh, but I will worry... unless you give me the five pounds now.' Elliot held his hand out. 'Come on, pay up.'

'People think you're so sweet and lovable—' I began.

He chuckled.

And he went on chuckling as I slipped five pounds into his hot, sweaty little hands.

**8.10 a.m.**
I'm the last to leave my house today. I'll be the first one back too, ready to meet *Dare to be Different* – with my alternative mum.

I really think this afternoon is going to change

74

my whole life. It's exciting living in such historic times.

**3.55 p.m.**
I'm back and already changed out of my uniform. Maddy's here too. She plonked down her sports bag, out of which she took a large bag of clothes. Her eyes sparkled. 'This is an adventure, all right.'

Then she raced upstairs to get changed. A few minutes later she returned. 'These shoes are a bit big for me. So I'll have to walk very carefully in them. But what do you think?'

She was wearing one of her sister's dresses, which was at least two sizes too big for her. But it was very bright red and eye-catching, as were her sister's dangly earrings. While perched on her head was that curly red wig. It was even bigger than I remembered. The whole look was perfect.

'Hello, Mum,' I smiled. 'I've missed you.'

**4.10 p.m.**
Maddy was glancing idly out of the window when she cried, 'Louis, there's a car going very slowly down your road. Now it's stopped. I think this IS IT.'

**4.40 p.m.**

It was.

Josh and Charlotte from *Dare to be Different* had arrived. Charlotte, who wore a polka dot neckerchief and white shirt combo, like a proper film buff, said to me, 'So happy to meet you, Louis. I've watched all your appearances on Noah and Lily now – and you are very funny, you know.'

We hit it off right away.

Meanwhile, Josh, small and bearded, quickly began setting up – he'd brought a webcam, exactly like the one Noah and Lily used. While he was doing that, Charlotte suggested asking me a few questions to 'warm us up'.

When I told her, 'I want to be a comedian more than anything,' Charlotte declared, 'That's excellent. We'll begin with you saying that,' adding, 'Just before we start, we do need a parent or guardian to sign—'

'Never fear, Charlotte,' I interrupted. 'My mum is very close by.' Listening right outside the door, in fact. 'Mum! Mum!' I called.

Immediately 'Mum' tottered in. She did have to walk extremely slowly in those shoes, but it all added to the effect. With a sweep of her arm Maddy declared, 'I bid you a warm welcome into our home,' in such grand, commanding tones she might have been a character in a costume drama. I felt proud of her already! 'I trust you had a good journey,' she went on. (Great touch that, as relics always prattle on about the journey, don't they?)

'Yes, thank you,' said Charlotte faintly.

'And the weather seems to have brightened up at last. Although all this rain has been so nourishing for the garden, hasn't it?' Maddy sounded so authentic, I felt like clapping.

Charlotte nodded very slowly before asking, 'You are Louis's mother?'

'I am indeed, my dear.' And then with brilliant timing Maddy let out an ear-splitting cough. It was even an improvement on the one she'd let go at the Belle Vue. In fact, the whole room seemed to shake with the force of it. Very unfortunately it also sent Maddy's wig tumbling down her forehead. But ever the pro, Maddy carried on as if nothing had happened. 'I have a lot of germs, which I don't want you to catch. So, shall I just sign your consent form before I go and lie down in a darkened room, and cough a lot.'

Neither Josh nor Charlotte replied at first. They were wide-eyed, staring right at Maddy. I really don't think they were expecting such a posh-sounding parent.

Then Maddy signed the form with one hand,

while straightening her wig, which was now in danger of escaping all the way down her face, with the other.

'Now, what light refreshment do you desire?' Maddy really had all the patter off.

Charlotte quickly replied, 'Nothing at all, thanks.'

So Maddy declared, 'Well, in that case, I'll bid you all a good afternoon and a safe journey home.' She then staggered out of the room, letting rip with another shattering cough before finally exiting.

Then there was silence – quite a long silence actually. Maddy had obviously made a big impression. In the end, I started asking Charlotte some questions about *Dare to be Different*. She told me it was very new. In fact, this was only their third interview, but they had big ambitions for the website.

'We are going to put your interview on so many media platforms,' said Charlotte. 'Josh is a genius with social media.' Josh actually grunted then. The most he'd said since he'd arrived. So even he must've been getting excited too.

**4.50 p.m.**
The interview began. I said, 'I want to be a comedian more than anything in the world,'

while grinning at Charlotte.

She grinned right back. Life looked very bright.

And that's when a car pulled up in the drive. I gawped at it in bewilderment.

It was Dad's car.

But he never haunted the family home so early on a Tuesday.

Except, apparently, TODAY. Nice one, Dad.

I jumped up, smiling hard at Charlotte. 'I'll be right back. Don't you dare go away, now.'

I charged to the front door, my heart beating out of my chest.

Now what was I going to do?

## Chapter Ten
# A Fast-acting Cold

Dad smiled at me. 'So, what do you think, Louis?'
I staggered back in total horror.

Dad was wearing the most horrible clothes in the known universe. He had on a ghastly purple jacket, which didn't even fit him properly as it was bulging at the seams, matching tight purple corduroy trousers, and his shirt was the brightest yellow I'd ever seen. He looked like Willy Wonka had thrown up custard on him.

Finally, for some obscure reason he was also sporting a pork pie hat.

'You haven't been to work dressed like that!' I exclaimed.

Dad chuckled. 'You young people are so

80

conventional – but no, I took the day off to go to Steve's open afternoon. You remember, he challenged us to wear some fun clothes to prove how unimportant our appearance is to us.'

'You've certainly proved that,' I said. 'And did... errr... Mum..?'

'Oh yes, she joined in too,' grinned Dad. 'One of her friends kindly took Elliot to the party. You know, Louis, we've had such a super time together searching the charity shops for clothes. Steve actually congratulated us for the way we entered into the spirit of things.'

I could only roll my eyes. I didn't trust myself to speak.

'Another really inspiring session with Steve too. We've got so much to show you.' Dad waved a carrier bag at me. 'Well, are you going to let me in?'

'I'm afraid not,' I jabbered at him. 'We have a very strict dress code here. Go away and find a jacket and tie...'

'Oh, stop being such a stick-in-the-mud.' Dad jostled past me good-naturedly. He seemed incredibly happy. So was this the moment to casually mention the *Dare to be Different* interview?

\* \* \*

**5.10 p.m.**

I was still considering that when the living-room door opened. Charlotte did a double take when she saw what Dad was wearing. But she quickly recovered and said very politely, 'Good afternoon.'

Dad's eyes widened so alarmingly that they were in danger of actually falling out of his head. 'Er, good afternoon, err…'

'I'm Charlotte and I'm here with Josh, and we're all ready to start, if that's all right with you? We shouldn't be in your way for very long.'

'I see,' said Dad absently, before asking, 'I'm very sorry, but who are you?'

'Charlotte just told you her name, Dad,' I said. 'Try and keep up. I know you've had a busy day trying on disgusting clothes—'

'Are you from Louis's school?' Dad interrupted. 'Is this some kind of project?'

'Yes, it's a kind of project,' I said desperately.

But Charlotte piped up. 'We're *Dare to be Different*, a new online show, and we're interviewing Louis for it.'

It was as if someone had flicked on a switch and Dad's tone instantly changed. 'Who gave you permission to do this?'

'Your wife,' said Charlotte. 'She has just signed our consent form, in fact.'

Dad wasn't expecting that. 'Oh, is my wife back from shopping already?' he faltered.

'Sure is,' I said.

'She went upstairs,' Charlotte added gently. 'I don't think she was feeling very well.'

A look of concern crossed Dad's face.

'A bad cold,' continued Charlotte softly.

'But she was absolutely fine when I left her,' spluttered Dad.

'It's one of those fast-acting ones,' I said quickly. 'One second you're bursting with health and the next you can hardly breathe. I think Mum just wanted to rest, didn't she?' I turned to Charlotte, who nodded in agreement. 'So, probably best if we don't disturb her.'

'But she definitely signed the consent forms. I can show them to you,' began Charlotte.

Dad hesitated.

I'd decided the top priority – the only priority – was to finish my interview. Explanations, and no doubt punishments, could follow later. So, I rushed on. 'While Mum is asleep, Dad, perhaps you could make us all a cup of tea?' Anything to keep him busy. 'Maybe you could throw in a biscuit or two, even a savoury option?'

Meanwhile, Josh had appeared in the doorway too.

'You can see they really want to start, Dad.' I

started to walk away from him. Was I actually going to get away with this? Perhaps the stars had finally aligned! Provided I moved extremely fast, it just might work. 'We'll let you get on with making the tea then, Dad. Bye.'

Suddenly a cough echoed down the stairs. Maddy had done this every so often to keep up the pretence – and because she was very proud of that cough.

'Yeah, Mum's got a bad cough as well,' I said. 'Just not her day, is it?'

But Dad strode to the top of the stairs and thundered, 'Whoever you are, come downstairs, immediately!'

'*Whoever you are?* What a way to talk to his wife,' I murmured to Josh and Charlotte.

A moment later, a door upstairs opened and then Maddy slowly thumped down the stairs, holding tightly to the bannisters as she did so.

'Hello again, everyone,' she said, then looking at Dad, 'And how are you, darling?'

What a performer – keeping in character to the very end. Just a shame Dad had to spoil it all by shouting, 'This is not Louis's mother!'

'Are you sure?' I asked him. 'Dad can be a bit absent-minded sometimes,' I explained to Charlotte.

'Of course it isn't,' said Dad with a grim laugh

and grabbing the wig right off Maddy's head. 'It's Maddy dressed up, because you both knew we'd never give you permission to do this.'

To say Charlotte and Josh looked really confused would be a massive understatement. They clearly hadn't a clue what on earth was going on. And any moment now, they'd start packing up. And another chance of stardom would be lost to me...

UNLESS... I made one last desperate bid to save the situation.

**5.30 p.m.**
'Dad, if you back down now, just this once,' I begged, 'and let me do the interview, well... I'll be grateful for at least eight centuries. So, as everyone is here and we'd already started, couldn't we finish? PLEASE?'

Dad didn't say anything for a long moment, then he let out a heavy sigh. 'Do you know who I really blame for this?'

'The government?' I suggested hopefully.

'You.' Dad pointed at a very startled Charlotte and Josh. 'You see, Louis is not himself at the moment.'

'Yes, I am,' I hissed indignantly. 'So, if I'm not myself, who am I?'

Dad lowered his voice confidingly. 'This is

not Louis's first encounter with the media. He featured regularly on Noah and Lily's vlog.'

'We know, we saw him,' said Charlotte.

'And you thought I was funny, didn't you?' I said.

But Charlotte didn't reply. She was pretending to be riveted by Dad's ramblings.

'What you may not know,' continued Dad, 'is that Louis was recently dumped by that vlog.'

*Dumped*! What a word to use in front of a comedian of my calibre. No wonder Maddy, who was now standing right beside me, gave my hand a quick squeeze. It wasn't true, either. I was let go. And that's totally different, isn't it?

'I can't tell you how upset he was.' Dad's voice was positively hushed now. 'We were both extremely worried about him—'

'No one wants to hear this, Dad,' I cut in.

But he continued, 'Louis had built his identity around becoming famous and making people laugh. He was chasing this dream all the time. So this rejection has thrown him off balance. We wanted to help Louis break free from this endless, joyless chasing after fame and show him there was so much more to life.'

Dad moved closer to Charlotte and Josh, all fired up now.

'Recently, my wife and myself started

attending a mindfulness class, in a spirit of some scepticism at first, but it has really helped us discover a sense of peace and enjoyment, and' – he smiled down at his hideous clothes – 'to be spontaneous and live in the moment. Well, we took Louis along to a family course on Saturday, hoping to steer him along on a similar journey of self-discovery. He resisted at first, as we knew he would. But this morning' – Dad's voice rose – 'Louis heard his mum and me practising our mindfulness breathing. And do you know what, he asked if he could join us—'

'That is so NOT true,' I interrupted. I turned to Maddy. 'Honestly, it isn't.'

'We were delighted,' said Dad. 'We felt we were really making progress, but now...' He sighed heavily.

'Of course, I understand,' said Charlotte, 'and we certainly won't go ahead with interviewing your son today.'

'Thanks a squillion, Dad,' I muttered. Maddy gave my hand another squeeze.

The next moment something totally jaw-dropping happened.

Charlotte asked Dad, '*Could we do an interview with you instead? Talking about mindfulness and how it's enriched your life?*'

## Chapter Eleven

# A Despicable Deed

I really thought I'd explode with shock. And when I finally recovered, I said, 'Good one, Charlotte – but how about we leave the jokes to me?'

Charlotte didn't answer. I could have been invisible. I was invisible. Instead she said imploringly to Dad, 'Our website gives people with a different perspective their chance to be heard. So we'd love to feature you talking about the value of mindfulness in the modern world.'

'And you really think people will want to hear what I've got to say?' asked Dad.

'I'm absolutely certain of it,' said Charlotte.

'And we're all set up,' said Josh, positively

chatty now, 'so it wouldn't take you very long.'

'Well, I'd want my wife to be on this too,' said Dad. 'She'll be here any minute... And I suppose you'd like me to change?'

'Oh no!' chorused Charlotte and Josh together. 'Don't change anything,' added Charlotte. 'Not even your hat – as I see it, it's all part of your story.'

'You're right, it is,' Dad agreed. 'And I suppose we have got a story to tell. So what exactly will I have to do?'

'We'll show you, sir,' said Josh. The next thing I knew, 'sir' had skipped after them both into the living room.

We stared after them, open-mouthed. 'Dad's really done it this time, Maddy,' I said. 'The ultimate despicable deed. He's nicked his own son's interview.'

Maddy agreed. 'He can't sink any lower.'

## Chapter Twelve
# Darkest Hour

**5.52 p.m.**
Mum has just arrived in a leopard-skin top, masses of silver jewellery and a huge cowboy hat. When Dad told her how he had robbed their oldest son of his interview, she frowned and said that she would talk to me later, as if I were the one who'd done something wrong!

Then, without any conscience at all, she followed Dad into the living room where they are getting ready to be interviewed. And now I have just heard them both laughing with Charlotte.

I might have even heard a chuckle from Josh.

\*　　\*　　\*

**6.05 p.m.**

The interview is still going on, and Maddy and I have been eavesdropping.

'Do you know what the worst part of this afternoon is?' asked Maddy.

'Hard to pick just one,' I said.

'Your mum and dad sound—' She struggled to put it tactfully.

'Even more boring than usual?' I cut in.

'Yes!' cried Maddy. 'It must be their voices – they're so dull and flat.'

I grinned. 'They sound like those automated voices you get on the phone. You know, press zero if you want to blow your nose, press one . . .'

'Yes, that's it exactly!'

'They make Daleks seem lively,' I continued. 'I suppose it's nerves changing their voices.'

'And I wish your dad wouldn't keep touching his face all the time, it's very distracting,' said Maddy.

'But he's an amateur, so he doesn't know stuff like that.'

We were silent for a moment, and then I said, 'Maddy, you don't suppose, well maybe, just maybe, *Dare to be Different* is pretending to be interested in all the rubbish my parents are spouting to keep in with them, so later they can pop back and interview me?'

91

'It's possible,' said Maddy, unconvincingly.

Then Elliot staggered towards us. 'I feel terrible,' he moaned.

'That'll teach you not to double cross me. And not to overeat at parties,' I added. 'You owe me five quid.'

'No I don't. I stayed at the party until half-past five. Not my fault if Mum wasn't there too. Plus,' he added, 'I've just been sick all over the kitchen floor.'

'Ergh. I Hope you've cleared it up,' I said.

'I can't,' he croaked unconvincingly.

'Why not?' I demanded.

'Far too ill. You'll have to do it, Louis. But you'll need to put on a mask as it really stinks. Bye.'

I turned to Maddy. 'Today just gets better and better.'

**6.30 p.m.**
Josh and Charlotte have gone. They just shouted 'Goodbye' at Maddy and me, not even waiting for us to reply. People in the media can be very fickle.

A second later, Maddy's parents stormed in and promptly went absolutely BALLISTIC, even though Maddy had kindly sent them a text, explaining exactly where she was. They said she was still under a 'strict curfew', as if we were in a war or something.

Next, Dad appeared. To my surprise, he tried to calm the situation down and even said Maddy had been 'an invaluable help' with an interview he and Mum had just given.

**6.38 p.m.**
That was good of Dad. But I know why he did it. He is racked with guilt – and so he should be.

**6.50 p.m.**
Mum has said that we must always tell them about any media interviews I am planning. 'And no more crazy stunts with Maddy,' added Dad. But that was it. No long lecture. Further proof of how guilty they are feeling, I thought.

But then they asked me if I had listened in to any of their interview, and when I said I had, they asked me what I thought.

'Well—' I began.

'It would be wonderful if our words helped people find more peace in their lives,' interrupted Dad eagerly. 'And we believe they might.' Then he and Mum exchanged gooey smiles.

So they had absolutely no idea how fantastically awful they were. What a shock they're about to get. This thought cheered me greatly.

**8.35 p.m.**

Isla has just texted to ask how my interview with *Dare to be Different* went – and when will it be available to watch. I am starting to go off my number one fan. She asks far too many questions.

**Wednesday April 30th**

**4.23 p.m.**

I was trudging home from school, when Isla sprang out of nowhere.

'I was hoping I'd spot you,' she said.

'Sorry I haven't answered your text yet,' I said.

'Don't worry, I only sent it last night.'

'Anyway,' I said quickly, 'my interview was postponed for various reasons too boring to talk about.'

'I am sorry, Louis.' She said it so sincerely, I grinned and asked, 'So how are you doing?'

'Well, Tiffany has invited me to her birthday party on Saturday. Of course, she'll be with Charlie – but she hopes there will be no hard feelings – and if I turn up on my own, that's not a problem. She's being revoltingly nice to me—'

'I'd definitely give it a miss then,' I interrupted.

'The thing is, just about every person I know

94

will be there.' Isla sighed. 'So I wondered if you'd do me a big, big favour.' She hesitated. 'No, it's too much to ask.'

'No harm in asking.'

'Would you walk into the party with me?'

'What, as your minder?'

'No, as my boyfriend.'

I quickly shook my head. 'I have a girlfriend.'

'I guessed you would have,' she said. 'And there wouldn't be anything in it. It's just if I walked into a party with a celebrity boyfriend, that would wipe the smug smiles off all their faces. You needn't stay very long – and I'd be ever so grateful to you.'

My heart sank. I always like to please fans, especially my number one fan. And I'd happily tell her jokes whenever she wanted. But to pose as her new boyfriend? That was asking too much. I couldn't do that.

So I said, 'I may be famous, but I'm nothing special in the looks department. I've bigger ears than Dumbo, for a start. So no guy is going to be jealous of me, and anyway... I really don't think you should go near that party – that's my advice.'

'And it's good advice,' she said very softly. 'The trouble is, I still like Charlie so much. Thanks for listening anyway. You're a nice guy, Louis...

Bye.'

'Look after yourself, Isla,' I called after her.

**4.40 p.m.**
Not home yet. Having a long, thoughtful walk instead. Fancy Isla wanting me to pretend to be her boyfriend. Impossible, of course. But when your career has hit rock bottom it's cheering to be asked.

**5.06 p.m.**
Home at last, where, to my surprise, I discovered Maddy. She was chatting to my putrid brother. After I'd evicted Elliot, she asked sympathetically, 'So which one of your teachers made you stay behind tonight?'

I could so easily have said, 'Actually I've been chatting with my number one fan – and you won't believe what she wants me to do.' And we could have had a bit of a chortle about it, but I didn't. Well, I wasn't going to be Isla's fake boyfriend, so what was the point of even mentioning it? Instead I muttered something vague about a total pain of a maths teacher and changed the subject. 'So your parents are letting you out again now?'

'Oh no, they're not, and they'll probably have another meltdown when they discover I haven't come straight home. But I don't care as they're already dishing out the WORST punishment ever, anyway!' She paused for a moment before hissing dramatically, 'They're only making me spend ALL Saturday and Sunday in the deepest Kent countryside with an ancient aunt who we hardly ever visit.'

'But why?'

'They think it will be very good for me to see something of the natural world for a change. But they're not staying there too. It will just be me and her... and a few cows.'

'Maddy, that's properly awful. You should write to your MP.'

'I think I will.'

'And I'm so going to miss you.'

She grinned. 'Anyway, I really came round to tell you that *Dare to be Different* have put up your parents' interview already.'

'That is the tragedy of my life,' I began. 'They're up on YouTube, being lame, and I'm here bursting with star quality, but—'

'Before you say any more,' interrupted Maddy, thrusting her phone at me, 'take a peek at your mum and dad's comments.'

I peeked. There were seven so far. The kindest one said: 'I had to keep watching because I couldn't believe how awful it was.' The others said stuff like: 'They were just so *dreadfully dull,*' and, 'Were they wearing those clothes and silly hats for a bet?' While one reflected glumly, 'That's twelve minutes of my life I'll never get back.'

I shook my head and said, 'What a surprise – not. No one has a good word to say about them.'

'Are you going to show it to them?' asked Maddy.

'You think I should?'

'Oh yes,' said Maddy eagerly. 'And you can stand right beside them, gloating away.'

'I can, can't I?'

'Do it now,' said Maddy. 'They're both in the kitchen.'

'I'll let you know what happens,' I announced. But I didn't move a muscle. Finally, I shook my head. 'They've done a very bad thing. But I can't do it. You see, they haven't an inkling how awful they were. They even thought their interview might help people.'

'They'll have to see it sometime,' said Maddy.

'Maybe.' I shook my head and said again, 'But I can't do it.'

'You spoil them,' said Maddy.

## Chapter Thirteen

# Helping My Number One Fan

**Thursday May 1st**

**8.03 a.m.**
The ping of two new texts woke me up. The first was from Edgar:

> I rarely watch videos on the internet, but I had an especially gruesome time viewing your parents. In fact, I ended up observing them from behind my hands. I sincerely hope Dare to be Different return to interview you. Remember our conversation about me venturing out more? Well, next time we

meet I may even have something to tell you.
Kind regards.
Edgar.

The other text was from Isla, who said she should never have asked me to pretend to be her boyfriend and only did so because she was very unhappy. She ended by saying she will always be my number one fan and is right now re-watching all my appearances on Noah and Lily's vlog.

**8.14 a.m.**
Isla's text has made me feel a bit mean. Especially as I think I would have made a dead good fake boyfriend.

**Friday May 2nd**

**4.25 p.m.**
Mum said, 'I suppose our interview for *Dare to be Different* will go up in about a week's time.'

'Yeeeah,' I said faintly.

'We figured that's how long it would take,' said Mum, from her and Dad's vast knowledge of the internet (they know absolutely nothing). 'Well, tell us when we hit the... errr... web, won't you?'

'Yeeeah,' I said, even more faintly.

'We were both very nervous during our interview,' Mum went on, 'but I don't think it showed much.'

I couldn't reply at all now.

**Saturday May 3rd**

**3.20 p.m.**
Mum and Dad told me they were going for a mindfulness walk. I think parents should be free to be as seriously mad as they wish – I'm very open-minded like that. So I merely nodded cheerily at them.

But then I realised, with horror, they meant for me to go with them.

**3.55 p.m.**
So Mum, Dad, Elliot and yours truly trudged to the park, pausing to admire a few dandelions on the way – and then settled down on one of the benches. Dad, after quickly glancing at one of Steve's pamphlets, announced, 'We're going to do some clapping first.'

'Why?' asked Elliot.

'Because it's fun,' lied Mum.

'We'll all do it together,' said Dad in his hearty voice. 'So come on, boys – one, two, three, that's it! Now keep clapping in time. Let's really keep it going now. Excellent – even louder, and do you see how this is energising us?'

A woman right ahead of us, whose Labrador was releasing a truly awesome amount of poo, suddenly whirled round. She obviously thought we were all clapping her dog's very lengthy ablutions, and shouted, 'There's no need to be so rude. And I will, of course, clean it all up.'

The clapping stopped immediately. Mum stared down at her shoes while Dad's face was all confusion. 'No, no, I assure you... we weren't...'

But anything else he said was drowned out by Elliot and me laughing.

And laughing.

The woman stalked away, waving the bag containing all her dog's offering at Dad as she did so.

'For a minute there,' I said, 'I thought she was going to bung that bag right at you, Dad.'

'Just imagine if she had,' cried Elliot, properly guffawing now. 'It would be dripping all down your face now and—'

'All right, boys,' interrupted Mum firmly. 'It wasn't as funny as that.'

'It so was,' I said, wiping my eyes on my jumper sleeve. 'So who shall we clap now?'

'I think we'll move on to some mind training,' said Dad solemnly.

**4.20 p.m.**
Our mind training involved looking at a leaf.
Yes, that's right – a leaf.

'Which one?' asked Elliot.

'Any one you like,' said Dad, indicating all the trees around us. 'And while you're staring at it, breathe slowly in and out too.'

'Only don't breathe near me,' I said to Elliot. 'Your breath stinks of cheese and onion crisps.'

Elliot promptly breathed right into my face.

'Stop it, you two,' said Mum. 'Open your minds to this.'

'But I'm hungry,' whined Elliot.

'Go and eat a leaf then,' I suggested.

'No more chatting,' said Dad. 'I want you to look carefully at your leaf – and see if you can notice something you've never spotted before.'

'It really is an incredible discipline for the mind,' said Mum.

There was silence. And Dad started doing his thoughtful face, which is very similar to the one he does when he can't find his car keys. Or when he needs the toilet.

'I don't know if anyone cares,' cried Elliot suddenly, 'but I've got a very sore bottom.'

I laughed.

'Have I really got to just look at a leaf?' he went on.

'OK, maybe we'll start you off with something else then,' said Dad. He pointed to a pigeon that was stalking about near our feet, on the lookout for any food. 'Tell me something about that bird, Elliot.'

Elliot considered. 'Pigeons poo on your head.' He started to laugh again. 'And they leave a white doo-doo behind.'

'The depth of his knowledge is astonishing,' I grinned.

'But what do you see here now, Elliot?' Dad persisted.

'That pigeon's very fat,' said Elliot. 'He should go on a diet.'

'And what about the way it moves? Study that,' suggested Dad.

'You know what, I actually think I'd rather look at a leaf,' said Elliot.

'Right, fine,' muttered Dad.

A whole two seconds went by before Elliot piped up again, 'Excuse me...'

'What?' snapped Mum and Dad together, sounding incredibly unrelaxed.

'Just to let you know that we're being watched,' Elliot hissed dramatically.

'Of course we're no—' began Mum.

But then she saw – we all saw – that we indeed were.

**4.50 p.m.**

A couple, who looked a bit older than Mum and Dad, wearing identical glasses perched on the middle of their noses, seemed to be absolutely fascinated by us. 'Hi there,' I called out to them. 'We're looking at leaves and fat pigeons. And it's great fun. Come and take my place – please.'

But they totally ignored me – their gaze was fixed on Mum and Dad.

'Very sorry for staring,' said the woman. 'I'm Enid and this is my husband, Malcolm. And we've just been watching you on YouTube.'

'Have you?' Mum and Dad sounded astonished.

'That must be our little interview,' said Dad, darting a glance at me.

I shifted awkwardly.

'One of our neighbours told us about it,' said Malcolm. 'He said you must watch this local couple – they're just so natural, and they will really cheer you up. Well, you certainly did that.'

'I wonder,' cut in Enid, 'would you mind if we have a picture with you? Or are we disturbing your…'

'No, of course not,' said Dad, jumping to his feet.

Enid thrust her phone in my direction. 'Thank you, dear,' she said absently, before shuffling over excitedly to Mum and Dad.

Five snaps later, Enid and Malcolm finally pottered off. And after that, mindlessness was completely forgotten, as Mum, Dad and Elliot were too busy staring at their phones.

'Why didn't you tell us our interview was up already?' Mum asked me.

'Well... er...' I began.

'He didn't tell you because he was jealous,' grinned Elliot.

'It's quite exciting, isn't it?' murmured Dad, and then his voice fell right away. Mum was completely silent too.

They were gaping at their comments.

I'd so been dreading this moment. I swallowed hard. What could I say? 'Yes, you were a bit rubbish, but it was very mean of people to point it out. Don't worry, though, I'm sure *Dare to be Different* will take it down soon and it will all be forgotten.'

All at once Dad began to laugh. I stared at him in alarm. The shock must have sent him temporarily insane. 'Well,' he declared, 'a few people didn't care for us – only to be expected, of course – but the vast majority were very flattering.'

What was he drivelling on about?

But then I noticed that since I'd last looked, tons of new comments had been added. And everything seemed to have completely flipped. One said, '*I love the way this couple don't care about how they're coming across, or what they're wearing. They're not putting on an act at all. They're so natural.*'

That word *natural* kept popping up. And *authentic*, and several people said they wanted to see more authentic people like this on YouTube.

'We've got 57 likes,' said Mum. 'Is that good, Louis?'

'Incredible,' I murmured.

**6.05 p.m.**
So I thought I'd be giving Mum and Dad a word of comfort about *Dare to be Different*, saying something like, 'You tried your hardest, so don't feel bad. But best to leave video appearances to professionals – like me.' Then I'd pat them on the shoulder in a really kindly way.

BUT INSTEAD, I'm the one who needs the kindly pat on the shoulder, as Mum and Dad have gained well over **a hundred** likes now. In fact, every time I look, the number jumps up again.

And you should see all their comments. One wrote, '*I loved them for not being slick and fake and just being themselves. They lifted my spirits.*' Someone else just said, '*They really cheered up*

107

*my day.'*

**6.08 p.m.**
So Mum and Dad's video is, for some obscure reason, entertaining the nation. And you know what that means, don't you? They haven't just nicked my interview – they are living my dream too.

**6.10 p.m.**
I so wish Maddy was here. I knew I would miss her this weekend. But I had no idea how much. And just before she left, her parents gave Maddy the awful news that they were not even sure if she will be able to get a mobile signal while she is away.

And we thought olden-days parents were bad sending their children up chimneys. But sending kids off to a place where there isn't even a mobile signal is far worse, isn't it? Maddy said she'd try her hardest to contact me somehow, but nothing from her yet.

**6.12 p.m.**
I suppose I could call Edgar. I've got to do something.

\*   \*   \*

**6.25 p.m.**

I've had another idea.

I texted Isla to say that I do like to help my fans, wherever possible. So yes, I will walk into the party with her, but only as her friend. Those were my terms.

Isla texted back within seconds to agree to my terms – and to say she always knew I wouldn't let her down.

## Chapter Fourteen

# Too Many Girlfriends

**Saturday May 3rd**
**7.00 p.m.**
So here I am, standing under a tree, at the top of Tiffany's road. This is where I'd arranged to meet Isla TEN – no, ELEVEN – minutes ago. And now the rain is bucketing down. So where is she? And how much wetter can I get?

**7.05 p.m.**
Quite a bit wetter, actually. In fact, it's raining so hard it feels as if someone is holding a hose over me. The good news is that I've had a text from Maddy, which I'm going to read right now. But, wait a second, I think I see Isla...

**7.24 p.m.**

It is Isla.

'I'm sorry, I'm sorry, I'm sorry,' she cries, tumbling towards me waving an umbrella about. We huddle under it.

'Louis, you're soaked,' she says.

'Well spotted.'

'This is so awesome of you. I only wanted to show Tiffany and' – her voice softens – 'Charlie that I don't care about them any more. So, I thought if they see me walk in with a superstar—'

'But he wasn't available, so you're stuck with Big Ears. I'm only going to poke my head in, say "Howdy" to your ex-best friend and ex-boyfriend, and then push off, if that's OK?'

'It's absolutely perfect,' says Isla. 'And anyway, Serena – she's my best friend now – always was really – has promised she'll be there, and she'll look out for me. You'll love her, by the way.'

I notice a small parcel under Isla's arm. 'You're not giving terrible Tiffany a present, are you?'

'Well, I had to bring something.'

'Why don't I go and collect some stinging nettles?'

She giggles. 'You're a great friend, Louis.'

'I try to be. Shall we head off to the party of the year then?'

She laughs very nervously and then says in a small voice, 'Why not?'

**7.40 p.m.**

'Lovely to see you again, Isla,' gushed Tiffany's parents. They were hovering by the front door, which is never a good place for parents to put themselves at a party, as it creates a terrible first impression. And actually, they didn't look so much pleased to see Isla as TOTALLY ASTONISHED.

Then they spotted the dripping figure beside her.

'Oh dear, is it still raining?' asked Tiffany's mum.

'No, I swam here,' I replied.

'This is Louis. He's a comedian,' said Isla proudly. 'He's been on Lily and Noah's vlog several times.'

'How splendid,' said Tiffany's mum vaguely.

'Might even tell you a joke later,' I said, 'if you're very lucky.'

But Tiffany's mum was far more interested in the parcel under Isla's arm. She whisked it away pretty quickly, as she wasn't allowing Tiffany to open any presents until her actual birthday, which turned out to be tomorrow.

Then Tiffany's dad spoke for the first time,

in a surprisingly deep, gravelly voice. 'You're just in time for the cutting of Tiffany's cake.' He made it sound at least as momentous as the Moon landing.

'Oh, goody good,' I cooed in a shrill, three-year-old voice. Isla giggled. Tiffany's mum turned away from us. 'Well, you should know your way around by now, Isla – you've been here often enough – so we'll leave you to join in the fun. I hope they've left you some refreshments!'

**7.41 p.m.**
They hadn't.

Well, except for a few shrivelled-up crisps. And you knew it was a bad party by the way everyone just wandered aimlessly around the large floral, old-fashioned living room and then into the kitchen – and then back again. No one actually settled anywhere.

I was already keenly looking forward to leaving. But I felt incredibly sorry for Isla. She kept smiling desperately at me, but I could tell what an ordeal this was for her.

Suddenly, Isla stiffened. 'Here they come,' she whispered. Gliding confidently through her guests came a small blonde-haired girl who looked positively angelic until she smiled. And then she just looked smug. Very, very smug.

113

'What a really wonderful surprise,' she cooed at Isla with blazing insincerity.

'Couldn't miss your birthday,' croaked Isla, and then quickly turned to me. 'And this is—'

'I know exactly who this is,' said an annoyingly good-looking, broad-shouldered boy, standing beside Tiffany. 'It's Louis the Laugh.'

He looked so genuinely happy, excited even, to see me that I actually felt embarrassed. 'Hi, how's tricks?' I muttered.

He grinned as if I'd said something incredibly funny. 'I'm Charlie and I've got to have a selfie with you, if that's all right. In fact, let's all be in it.'

So we had a selfie, Tiffany looking considerably less enthusiastic than everyone else. And when Charlie started gibbering on about how he and Isla never missed an edition of Noah and Lily's vlog when I was on it, the smile actually fell off Tiffany's face for a few seconds.

She didn't like all these reminders of when Isla and Charlie were together. That's probably why Tiffany suddenly started holding hands with Charlie – and dribbling on about how she couldn't wait for tomorrow to see what lovely presents Charlie had bought her.

'I may throw up,' I whispered to Isla, 'all over her lovely presents.'

But she didn't smile. Instead, Isla burst out, 'Well, I've got some news too – wonderful news. Louis the Laugh has asked me out – and I've accepted.'

I gulped more than once. What on earth was Isla doing? This wasn't what we'd agreed at all. But it had certainly shut up Tiffany and Charlie. They were both gawping at us.

'I had no idea it was so serious,' murmured Charlie.

'It really is,' began Isla, her cheeks aglow. She was most convincing. 'We're just so very happy, aren't we, Louis?'

I was saved from saying anything by a tall, untidy-looking girl charging over to us. 'Did I hear right?' she screeched. 'Has a boy been mad enough to ask you out?' She grinned at me. 'Hi, Louis, I'm Serena and I just want you to know Isla will make you an epic girlfriend. She's always talking about you too.' She flashed a glance at a distinctly shocked-looking Charlie. 'And she deserves some happiness with you, Louis, after what she's been through lately. She really does.'

The next thing I knew Isla and Serena were hugging each other. I stood there struggling with a nightmarish feeling of horror. Where was this going? I should walk out right now.

**7.56 p.m.**

I very nearly did. Only I knew that would totally humiliate Isla in front of Tiffany and Charlie.

So instead, I hissed, in a voice which indicated I was not my usual sunny self, 'Isla, can I have a word with you, like right now?' But my words were drowned out by the gravelly tones of Tiffany's dad, urging everyone to gather round, as the moment of heart-stopping excitement had arrived. They were cutting the cake!

Everyone from the kitchen swarmed in too. I spotted someone walking as straight as a soldier on parade. But he also looked dazed and confused as if he couldn't quite believe he was there. He wasn't the only one. It was truly a shock to see Edgar at a social gathering! He'd said something about going to a party, now I thought about it. But why on earth did it have to be this one?

I looked across at Isla and Serena, still babbling away together. Isla mustn't meet Edgar again. Especially after what she'd just announced. That would... I didn't even want to finish that sentence.

I was definitely bailing out now. Only, at that very moment, all the lights were switched off. 'Hope you're all in good voice,' cooed Tiffany's mum. I looked wildly around me. I had to hide from Edgar. But where? I dived down behind the sofa where I was certain no one would see me. It was a pretty good hiding place actually, even if it was a bit cramped.

Above my head a distinctly half-hearted rendition of 'Happy Birthday' wafted past (I wondered how popular Tiffany actually was). This was followed by a mad scramble for cake.

I peeped out cautiously, then slowly emerged from behind the sofa, like a particularly shy snail. Where had Edgar gone? I quickly spotted him, standing in the cake queue and looking exactly as if he were waiting to do an exam. He was talking to someone too. Wow! Well done, Edgar. And then I saw who it was.

Hot and cold tremors ran up and down my spine. No, that was impossible. I'd been thinking about her so much today and wishing she was here – somehow I'd conjured her up.

She was a mirage. People were always getting them in deserts. Now I was having one at a party. And when I blinked she'd vanish away.

So I blinked and waited.

But amazingly she didn't budge.

IT WAS MADDY!

## Chapter Fifteen
# Louis's Double Life

**8.01 p.m.**
So I immediately dived behind that sofa again. It seemed the safest place. And it was then that I did something incredibly stupid.

I sneezed. Twice.

They were dead loud sneezes too. More like little explosions. So it wasn't very surprising when two boys popped their heads over the sofa, and then pointed at me. 'Ha-ha,' they said.

'Ha-ha,' I replied, hoping after a few more ha-has, they'd clear off. But instead I became something of an attraction. And soon heads were bobbing up all over the sofa. 'What are you doing down there?' asked one girl.

'Not a lot,' I replied.

'You're Louis the Laugh,' called a boy so loudly, I winced. Then he added, 'Is it your mum and dad who are all over the internet?' I was attracting more attention here than if I was strolling about. And the very last thing I wanted was Maddy and Edgar discovering me lurking behind a sofa. That would look incredibly suspicious.

So, I did the only thing I could, I stretched and clambered to my feet. 'That's so refreshing,' I announced to the large audience gawping at me. 'You ought to try it some time.' Most other people were still clustered round the free cake. One girl was even complaining loudly about the slow service.

**8.15 p.m.**
I was streaking towards the door when I heard, 'Louis! We're over here!'

Pushing her way out of the cake queue came a grinning Maddy, closely followed by Edgar.

'Great you could make it,' she cried, sounding just as if she'd been expecting me to come here. I couldn't understand that at all.

'I know my text was insanely confusing,' Maddy rushed on. The text I still hadn't read, of

119

course. 'But it's been such a chaotic day. Can you believe we had to travel all the way to my aunt's house before we found out her pipes had burst? My parents were in such a foul mood after that and the journey back took forever as well. So I really didn't think they'd let me out tonight – and certainly not to see you' – she smiled at me – 'as you're such a bad influence.'

'I do my best,' I grinned sheepishly.

'It was only at the very last minute that they agreed to me going to this party with Edgar. He persuaded them. Anyway, that's why my text was so rushed.' Maddy peered at me anxiously. 'You look very hot.'

'Ha-ha.' Yes, I was back to saying that again. I swiftly changed the subject. 'So, Edgar, what's more fun – coming to this party or eating a bucket of snot?'

'I fear the bucket of snot would have the edge,' said Edgar gravely. 'But at least I have proven to myself that I can endure occasions such as this.'

All the time I was talking, I was looking around, and to my huge relief I couldn't see any sign of Isla. But I really didn't want to push my luck. So I said, 'As it's such a spectacularly awful party, shall we go?'

'I will give up the doubtful pleasure of rejoining the queue for cake, if you will, Maddy?' said Edgar.

Maddy smiled in agreement.

And we were just about to leave, when a voice behind me said, in a confiding whisper, 'Your girlfriend is outside, Louis, and I think she'd like to see you.'

I whirled round to see Serena smiling anxiously at me.

This was awful.

No, far, far worse than awful.

Neither Maddy nor Edgar moved or spoke.

Noticing their stunned faces Serena gave me a conspiratorial grin. 'So... you haven't told them yet?' she added helpfully. 'Well, he only asked her out tonight.'

Maddy and Edgar went on doing their impression of two stunned goldfish, while I couldn't think of a single thing to say. My brain had seized up with horror.

It was Maddy who spoke at last, in a faint faraway voice. 'So what is the name of Louis's new girlfriend?'

'Isla,' smirked Serena. 'And she's so thrilled about—'

'Did you say Isla?' Edgar suddenly interrupted.

'Why, do you know her?' demanded Maddy at

once.

Edgar went bright red. 'Well... I have made her acquaintance on one brief occasion.'

'She's lovely, isn't she?' gushed Serena.

'When was this?' Maddy's voice was slowly rising, while Edgar's face went even redder, if that were possible.

He explained. 'I saw her and Louis taking pictures of each other...'

'One picture,' I murmured. 'A selfie.'

'And where were you, Edgar?' Maddy demanded.

'At the time I was' – he paused – 'taking some litter out of the bins and then putting it back in again.'

Now it was Serena's turn to look confused. 'But why on earth were you doing that?'

'Well, I've observed a lot of rubbish falls out of bins because it's been deposited incorrectly, so I—'

'Edgar,' interrupted Maddy softly, gently. 'Stop talking – now.' Then she looked right at me. 'So it seems you have two girlfriends now!'

I smiled. 'Now, come on, folks, is this the face of a boy with two girlfriends... or is it the face of a boy with one girlfriend? Well, only if he's very, very lucky.' I laughed lots and lots. No one else laughed at all.

And Serena demanded accusingly, 'Do you already have a girlfriend then?'

'Yes – Maddy!' I cried.

'And does Isla know about – her?' Serena was cross-examining me now.

'Of course she does,' I said.

'So you've been talking about me with her, have you?' asked Maddy.

'Well, a bit. Not much. Look, the thing is, I was doing Isla a good deed.'

'Think a lot of yourself, don't you?' snapped Serena. 'Just because you used to be on a vlog.'

'I think,' said Edgar slowly, 'you ought to find Isla immediately and sort out this misunderstanding.'

'There's nothing to sort out,' I protested. 'I've been helping Isla, that's all.'

'Well, you'd better go on helping her, hadn't you!' shouted Maddy. 'Enjoy yourself,' she added bitterly.

'Maddy!' I cried desperately. 'Do you have any idea how much I've missed you today?'

Maddy gave the most unamused laugh I'd ever heard before darting into the party again.

Edgar shook his head at me. 'I'm extremely sorry, Louis, that you involved me in your deception.' He quickly followed Maddy.

I was left with Serena looking daggers at

me. 'Are you going to see poor Isla or not?' she demanded.

'Oh yes,' I replied. 'And I have a lot to say to "poor Isla".'

## Chapter Sixteen

# Living the Dream
# (Mum and Dad, That Is)

**8.25 p.m.**
Only Isla wasn't outside.

'The poor girl's probably gone home,' announced Serena. She gave me a horrible look before adding, 'I think all boys stink.' After that cheery observation, she left me on my own.

I tore back into the party. Tiffany's parents were clapping their hands and shouting, 'Come on, everyone, time to get dancing.' Everyone was very sensibly ignoring them completely. I did a quick circuit of the whole party but no sign at all of Maddy or Edgar. Surely they hadn't sloped off without even giving me a chance to explain. But it seemed they had.

Then a face loomed up next to me.

'Where's Isla?' demanded Tiffany.

'Haven't a clue,' I muttered.

'But why don't you know?' she shrieked at me. 'She's your girlfriend.' Which struck me as pretty rich coming from her.

I left after that.

**8.40 p.m.**

It had stopped raining, but it was a grey, cheerless night and I was still trying to figure out what to do next, when a voice said, 'Good evening.' Without even looking up, I knew who that was.

'Why didn't you wait at the party for me, Edgar?'

'Maddy wanted to leave right away.'

'How is she?'

'Very quiet... and I think she wants to be quiet for a while longer. That's why I've left her at her house. She gave me a message for you, though.'

'I'm all ears... I mean, I really am.' I was trying to make a joke, but my heart was thumping like crazy.

'Maddy doesn't want you to phone, text or

go around and see her. I expect she will wish to communicate with you at some point in the future, but definitely not tonight...' He paused. 'May I ask you a question?'

'Go on.'

Edgar swallowed very hard. 'Have you been living a double life?'

'No, of course not,' I shouted. 'I only went along tonight because you can't just ignore your fans, can you?'

'Please explain,' said Edgar.

After I'd told him everything, he said, 'Isla should have stayed right away from that party. Not turn up, parading you around like some show pony. That may be the stupidest idea of all time.'

'Don't hold back, Edgar,' I said.

'May I offer you a suggestion?' he asked.

'Go for it.'

'Allow me to tell Maddy your explanation – and wait for her to contact you.'

I considered this. 'OK. Do your best for me, won't you?'

Edgar gave me his idea of a reassuring smile, before the night swallowed him up.

**10.05 p.m.**
My phone beep-beeped. Got very excited. I knew

Maddy would understand the difficult position I was in. What a girlfriend.

And then I saw my text was from Isla.

It said:

I should NEVER have said you were my boyfriend. Can you ever forgive me? Please, please do, because it worked. Charlie said how jealous he felt seeing me with you. Can you believe he actually walked out of Tiffany's party to tell me that? Thank you. Thank you, thank you, Louis - always your number one fan.

## Sunday May 4th

**2.00 p.m.**
Still not a beep from Maddy. But Edgar rang.

'Maddy has said she will probably contact you.'

'Only probably?' I was very disappointed.

'She had a big shock last night,' said Edgar sternly. 'In fact, I never expected her to take it so well.'

'OK. Well, listen, if you do see Maddy, tell her it's completely up to her when she calls and there's no rush at all. But would she hurry up as I hate us not talking.'

**5.10 p.m.**

'What do you do if you find a python in your toilet? *Wait until he's finished.* And what did—' But I stopped there. Dad was hovering in my bedroom doorway.

'Telling jokes to yourself?' he asked.

'No, Dad, I'm practising my comedy act. Something I do every single night.'

'Yes, of course you do,' said Dad absentmindedly, before plonking himself on the edge of my bed. 'Have you seen how many likes your mum and I have got now?' he asked.

Actually, I'd stopped looking – well, I was far too worried about Maddy for a start – but I could guess. 'Still rocketing up?' I guessed.

Dad nodded incredulously. 'Have to share with you one comment that's just appeared.' He fiddled with his phone for a moment before reading out: '"*I've felt miserable and fed up recently, but this video – so completely natural and unspun – has left me with a smiling face. Thank you.*" What about that, Louis?'

I'll tell you what about that. It so wasn't fair. I mean, while my parents were lifting the nation's spirits, what have I been doing? Going to a horrible party and falling out with my girlfriend.

But, somehow, I managed to bleat heroically,

'That's a marvellous compliment, Dad.'

'Isn't it?' His face was one big, amazed smile.

And I was glad he was happy. I just wished he'd skip away and be very happy somewhere else. But instead he hung about for ages, gibbering away excitedly about it all.

Parents can be so inconsiderate.

**7.05 p.m.**
The doorbell rang. Elliot raced to answer it before announcing in a bored voice, 'It's only Maddy.'

This news sent me leaping downstairs. 'Hey, Maddy!' And in case she missed that sparkling jewel of conversation, I went, 'Hey, Maddy!' again. 'Come in, come in.' I didn't know why I was saying everything twice. (Yes I do. I was very, very nervous.)

Dad was rabbiting away on the phone in the living room, so we went into the kitchen. Normally Maddy would immediately make herself at home, but today she hung by the kitchen door as if she hadn't ever been in my house before. I'd never felt so shy with Maddy. So I started gabbling away.

'Now I've got an uncle who I only ever see at Christmas, and every time we meet up he asks me the same question, "How are you diddling?"

130

So, Maddy, how are you diddling? And sit down for goodness' sake.'

Maddy perched on the edge of the chair nearest the door, then said softly, 'I've spoken to Edgar.'

'And he's told you what really happened.'

She nodded very slowly.

'Well, here's the big question. Do you believe him – well, me, really? I'm getting confused now. But you know what I mean?'

'Yes – and I do.'

I let out a huge sigh of relief. 'That's fantastic, because I can see how it's a bit muddling, having another girl racing about saying she's my girlfriend. You must have asked yourself what was going on—'

'Louis,' Maddy interrupted, 'I think we should take a break.'

'What?' I was too choked to say anything else, but finally I managed to croak out, 'Why?'

'Because, Louis, I think you're getting tired of me.'

'That's so not true.'

'Edgar said Isla was a very pretty girl,' she continued.

'Cheers, Edgar.'

'No, I wanted all the facts, especially as I've never actually met her. She is pretty, isn't she?'

'I suppose so.'

'And you took her to a party?'

'No, I didn't take her. I walked in next to her. And I only did it because she's a fan – although I shan't ever offer this service to fans any more, I can promise you that.'

Maddy stood up. 'I'm not dumping you – I shall continue to watch your career with considerable interest.'

'What career?' I mumbled.

'And will you promise me something?'

'Anything.'

'You'll keep practising your comedy every single night.'

'But it won't be the same without you. I mean, look at the way you helped me get into that hotel room to see Marcus Capel. I'd never, ever have done that on my own.'

For a moment, Maddy smiled reminiscently. 'That was brilliant fun... just a shame he wasn't the right one. Maybe you'll have better luck without me.'

'I'll have no luck at all. Maddy, please don't go.'

She actually hesitated. And then, at the worst possible moment Dad, Mum and Elliot burst in, looking all merry and bright. 'Sorry to interrupt, guys,' said Mum. 'And how are you,

Maddy?' Without waiting for a reply she rushed on, 'We've got some really astonishing news for you.'

'They've found Elliot's one brain cell,' I quipped, just wanting them to all go – fast.

But Elliot didn't even punch me. Instead he cried triumphantly, 'Mum and Dad are going to be superstars!'

## Chapter Seventeen
# Viral Sensations

**7.45 p.m.**

'Now, don't get carried away, Elliot,' said Mum. But she was buzzing. All three of them were. What on earth was going on?

'You tell them,' Mum said, turning to Dad.

'Hold onto your hats, guys,' cried Dad. 'I've just been having a chat' – he paused significantly – 'with the researcher from *Live at Five*.'

'You can't mean,' I yipped, 'the television show called—'

'The very same,' interrupted Dad. 'I thought it was someone playing a joke on us, at first, especially as the researcher sounded about twelve. And when she said they want your mum

134

and me to appear on it tomorrow, I nearly passed out with shock.'

'What exactly do they want you to do?' I asked, flabbergasted.

'You know they have a spot on it called, "What's Hot, on the Internet?"'

Of course I did. Hadn't I seen Noah and Lily on that very spot a few days ago?

'We'll be on that part,' Dad chuckled. '*Just be your wonderful, natural selves.* Those were the researcher's exact words. And I suppose we'll be talking about what we said on *Dare to be Different*. And, oh yes, they've even asked us to wear exactly the same clothes we wore during our interview.'

'And will Clive be interviewing you?' I asked.

'Do you know, I think they said he would.' Dad shook his head in amazement.

'We still can't believe any of it,' cried Mum. 'Or why they want us.'

'We're refreshingly different,' grinned Dad triumphantly. 'That's how the researcher described your mum and me. What about that?' Then he looked across at Mum, who nodded. 'Louis, we'd be really grateful if you came with us tomorrow.'

'Why on earth do you want him?' demanded Elliot. 'He's not refreshingly different.'

'We'd really appreciate his help tomorrow,' Dad said firmly. 'Well, Louis knows so much more about show business today than we do. Not to mention performing.'

'You'll only need to leave school a few minutes early, if that's what's worrying you,' said Mum. 'They're sending a car for us.'

'Trust me, it's not… Of course I'll come along, thanks.'

Then the doorbell rang and Maddy and I were on our own again.

'Wow,' I said. 'Never saw that coming – can you believe it, my mum and dad appearing on *Live at Five*?'

Maddy, who had been oddly silent when Mum and Dad were telling us the news, didn't say anything at first. Finally, in a voice hardly above a whisper, she said, 'Just to let you know, I shan't be taking a break from you tonight after all.'

'Thanks a zillion, Maddy.'

'I shall wait until next weekend.' And before I could reply, she'd gone.

**Monday May 5th**

**7.15 a.m.**
Woken up by stinky breath all over my face. At

first I thought it must be a dog, which was a bit puzzling, as we don't have a dog. But then Elliot bellowed into my ear, 'You've got to be really, really quiet.'

I blinked up at him. 'And you're going to be really, really punched. What are you even doing in my bedroom?'

'I had to tell you,' said Elliot, oozing self-importance, 'not to make any sounds at all when you go downstairs, as Mum and Dad are being interviewed by the local radio right now. Isn't that brilliant?'

'If you say so.'

Elliot settled himself on my bed. 'Who would have thought it! Our parents on *Live at Five*! I mean, you were a little bit famous once, I suppose. But Mum and Dad are very, very famous now, aren't they?'

'Elliot, would you like me to sit on your head?'

'And it's so kind of Mum and Dad to let you tag along with them today. At least you can watch them being really famous, can't you?' He darted to the door, farted and left.


**2.30 p.m.**
I hurtled out of school just as a vast car pulled up. The front passenger door swung open. 'Can we offer you a lift to the TV studios?' chuckled

Dad, leaning out of the rear window.

'We thought you'd like to sit in the front,' added Mum, as if I were about two. They were both sitting in the back and wearing those revolting clothes again.

The car glided off, whisking us away to TV land. An enchanted place, whose doorway was suddenly (incredibly) opening – for Mum and Dad.

**3.50 p.m.**
We were met by a tall girl waving a clipboard. She was called Nina, and smiled relentlessly.

'We're very excited, Nina,' confided Dad.

'So are we,' she cried. 'Everyone thinks you're just so unspoilt and real.'

She led us through some double doors and down a very long corridor. 'Here's the green room,' she announced. Of course, it wasn't green – they never are – but it contained two couches, tea and coffee machines, and a basket crammed with miniature bars of chocolate. And on the wall was a large television.

'I just need a bed and I could move in here,' I quipped.

**4.16 p.m.**
Nina has taken Mum and Dad to make-up. 'We may be gone some time,' joked Dad.

'Speak for yourself,' laughed Mum. They were in such high spirits, they might have been setting off on holiday. That surprised – and worried – me somehow.

Moments after they'd gone, a waft of expensive perfume entered, followed by a heavily made-up woman, who made herself comfortable on the other couch. She told me she was Greta the Garden Guru and was here for the 'Get Out into the Garden' slot, and then she asked me who I was.

'Great question,' I grinned. 'I'm Louis, Louis the Laugh, and I'm with my mum and dad. Only they're not here right now, as they've gone to be plastered with make-up—'

'Oh, you're a civilian,' she interrupted. I must have looked puzzled as she went on, 'A civilian is someone who isn't in show business – and personally I'd say you are very lucky indeed. It can be so stressful and demanding.' She sighed heavily. 'As I know all too well.'

Before I could correct her truly terrible error – a civilian, indeed! – Greta's agent swept her off to have her picture taken next to a cactus or something.

**4.20 p.m.**
A text from Maddy:

**It should be you on Live at Five. Not sure I can even watch it, though I probably will. Maddy**

How thoughtful. Then I noticed something awful. Maddy always ends her texts with 'x' but today the 'x' was missing. She might have forgotten, of course. Only she's never forgotten before.

**4.21 p.m.**
Here's a terrible thought. What if that missing 'x' means: *I feel sorry for you, but I still intend to take a break from you as soon as I can.*

**4.33 p.m.**
I was reciting jokes to try to cheer myself up after that missing 'x', when Mum and Dad returned, their faces glistening with make-up. Right behind them bounded an enthusiastic, bustling guy, with a beautifully manicured beard and wearing round, black-rimmed glasses.

'Hi, folks, how are you doing? I'm Mitchell, the show's producer. Just wanted to tell you that you're on first. And we know you'll get our show off to a fantastic start.' He didn't seem to notice that Mum and Dad had suddenly started deflating, like two burst balloons.

'You're being interviewed by Clive,' Mitchell

continued, 'and he's looking forward to having a bit of fun with you.'

'Fun?' croaked Dad, as if that was a word he'd never heard in his life before.

'Clive wondered if you'd had any amusing experiences while performing mindfulness?' asked Mitchell.

Dad looked alarmed. 'Well, I can't think of any, to be honest. I wasn't expecting you to ask us anything like that.'

'There was that time in the park,' I suggested, 'when we were clapping, and that woman thought you were clapping her dog doing his—'

'I don't think so,' interrupted Mum firmly.

'Not to worry,' grinned Mitchell. 'Leave it all to Clive, and just be your usual, authentically wacky selves.'

'Wacky,' echoed Mum disbelievingly. 'I don't think anyone has ever described us like that before.'

Mitchell laughed. 'You're going to have the best time, guys. And Nina will be back very soon to mike you up.'

After he'd bounced off, a heavy silence settled over the green room. Mum and Dad seemed lost in thought. 'Sounds ace, doesn't it, being interviewed by Clive?' I said at last. 'Like a dream really.'

'That's it exactly,' said Dad. 'Like a dream. And I think I've just woken up. What on earth am I even doing here?' He turned to Mum. 'There's no way we can go through with this, is there?'

'I'm so glad you said that.' The words seemed to erupt out of Mum like a volcano, and even under the powder her face gleamed bright red.

'You've got all these butterflies fluttering about inside your stomach,' I said cheerily. 'Don't worry, everyone gets them. It's very natural – and good really.'

'Not like this,' said Dad.

'I'm absolutely shaking inside,' cried Mum.

'I wish I were one of those people who thrives on appearing on television,' said Dad, 'but all my instincts are telling me I am not. We have no business being here – we're imposters.'

At that moment, a beaming Nina returned. 'We're all ready for you to be miked up now.'

Dad couldn't have looked more horrified if Nina had been a dentist, brandishing a massive drill. But it was Mum who spoke. 'Will you do us a favour, please, Nina?'

'Of course,' she smiled.

'Please,' asked Mum, her voice rising, 'order us a taxi home RIGHT NOW?'

## Chapter Eighteen
# Guru Louis

**4.45 p.m.**

Nina reeled, and even though I was sitting down, I did a bit of reeling too.

'We will, of course, refund your travel costs,' said Mum. 'And we're very sorry to have messed you about like this, but it really is for the best.' She lowered her voice confidingly. 'We're not at all wacky, you know.'

Dad nodded. 'You'll have a much better show without us amateurs... so we'll just slip away now. Thank you for the huge compliment of inviting us.'

'And it's been so lovely meeting you,' added Mum.

There was a pause. Clearly nothing like this had ever happened on *Live at Five* before. No wonder Nina looked like an actress who had forgotten every one of her lines.

Meanwhile, I know you are asking yourself, what was I doing all this time?

Very simple.

I was gloating.

I was laughing a bit too. Not out loud, of course. But in my head I was going, 'Heh, heh, heh,' while thinking, 'That'll teach them to steal my interview.'

Yes, I was mean. Yes, I was bitter. But then another voice inside my head piped up: 'Dad was right. He and Mum are only amateurs. But you're not. And you know what's happening to them. They're letting their nerves take them over... That's why they are acting like immature adults now. It's just lucky they've brought an un-immature kid with them – who can't let them go hurtling back to obscurity!'

And I couldn't.

So I stopped gloating and going, 'Heh, heh, heh,' in my head and said to Nina, 'This is only a little blip. Mum and Dad are very artistic, you know. But I promise you they'll be ready to be miked up soon.'

'We really won't,' said Mum at once.

'They really will,' I said firmly. 'Could you give us a few minutes please, Nina?'

Nina could.

As soon as she'd gone, I tried to explain to my parents about nerves. But they weren't listening to me. Mum even said she was off to find Nina and it wasn't fair on *Live at Five* to drag this out.

What on earth could I do now?

It came to me in a flash.

A truly mad idea.

But it was my only hope.

I immediately dived down onto the floor and sat cross-legged.

'Louis, what on earth are you doing?' asked Dad.

'Get up at once,' snapped Mum.

'Join guru Louis,' I smiled up at them, 'for my exclusive mindfulness course.'

'Don't be ridiculous,' said Mum.

'Come on,' I cried. 'You're always saying how great mindfulness is. Well, let's try it now. What have you got to lose?'

'But what are you going to do?' demanded Mum.

'Join guru Louis and find out,' I said.

Dad was suddenly amused. 'You're wasting your time – but I'm always ready to practise some mindfulness. And our son instructing us will certainly be a novelty.' To my huge relief, he, and a very reluctant Mum, joined me on the floor.

'What on earth are we doing?' asked Mum.

'No talking in guru Louis's class, please,' I replied. 'All together now, breathe in and relax.' I said this in such a perfect imitation of the way Dad always said it that he burst out laughing. 'Next, hold your breath…

'We know how to do it,' snapped Mum.

'Got some right know-alls in my class, haven't we?' I said.

Dad chuckled. 'Better follow our guru.'

They were soon breathing away. Then I said, 'Well done. Now we're going to really get the party started and make with the *Oms*. Now what's the matter?' I asked Mum, who was scowling at me.

'You're saying *Om* like *Um*,' said Mum, 'which is completely wrong.'

'How dare you challenge the guru – show me, then,' I cried.

So Mum did. 'See how I'm opening my mouth widely and letting the word echo through my body, Louis?'

Dad threw in a really long *Ommmm* too. They really were a pair of show-offs.

So I had another go.

'It still sounds too much like *Um...*' cried Mum.

She and Dad were off again, closing their eyes now and spouting *Ommmm*. And soon there was no stopping them. They were still in mid *Ommmm* when the door opened. Nina, seeing us all sitting on the floor, let out a startled gasp.

I jumped up. 'Don't worry, they're ready to talk about mindfulness, after my crash course. I taught them everything they know.'

Dad looked up at me for a moment, then, still grinning, sprang to his feet. After helping Mum up, he declared, 'For some reason I do feel better about it all... and after all, what have we got to lose but our dignity?'

'I wouldn't worry,' I quipped. 'You lost that years ago.'

Mum and Dad exited holding hands, which was kind of cute in a yucky sort of way.

Just before she left, Mum whispered to me, 'It's only thanks to guru Louis we're going on at all.'

'That's right – blame me,' I grinned.

MUM + DAD

## Chapter Nineteen
# Living with Superstars

**4.55 p.m.**
Just been shown to my seat in the front row. And the studio is so much smaller than I expected. There can't be more than two hundred people packed in here. No wonder the warm-up guy, Jasper, keeps telling the audience to make a lot of noise.

I've heard most of Jasper's jokes before. They weren't very funny the first time. But he's got personality, I'll give him that. And the audience can't get enough of him.

**5.04 p.m.**
Clive appears and immediately gets a huge

laugh, as he is wearing very tight-fitting yellow shorts. He stands there shaking his craggy face, while the laughter goes on and on.

'I know, I've put you off your tea,' he says at last. 'In fact, after seeing my knees, you may never want to eat again. But they made me do it.' He leans forward. 'They said I had to dress like this to make this week's viral internet sensations feel at home.' Clive continued, 'Our first guests are a couple who say clothes are totally unimportant and don't care what they wear – as you will now see.'

A little shiver runs through me as I realise he is talking about Mum and Dad. My parents are about to be seen by *millions*.

**5.10 p.m.**
Mum and Dad totter jerkily up the steps. They are moving like two huge puppets. And then Dad trips. He only just stops himself from falling over. I'm not the only one in the audience to gasp. Clive, who is waiting at the top of the stairs, dashes forward and offers Dad a hand. 'It was the sight of me in those yellow shorts, wasn't it?' he quips.

'No,' replies Dad. 'I'm just very, very nervous.' This gets a big 'aaah' from the audience.

**5.13 p.m.**

Mum and Dad are telling everyone about their journey to find the 'stillness within'. Only, Dad's voice has gone all flat and lifeless again. While Mum's voice is travelling up and down like a roller coaster, soft one moment, then very loud indeed.

I want to rush up and do something – anything – to help them relax and let themselves go a bit.

Then Dad seizes up in the middle of a sentence. 'Sorry, I got lost there. We actually made some cards with everything we wanted to say, but somehow, we forgot them. Very sorry, everyone.'

There are stifled sniggers all around me and Clive tries desperately hard not to laugh too. Actually, Clive is really playing up to the audience. Mum and Dad aren't as bad as all that.

**5.14 p.m.**

Yes they are.

**5.15 p.m.**

Now Clive is sitting cross-legged on the stage with Mum and Dad either side of him. 'Come on then, teach me how to say *Om*,' he says.

'This will make you feel so relaxed,' begins Mum. But the next moment she starts to cough, and stutters, 'Water, need water now.'

Clive leaps up, pours water into a glass, accidentally (or maybe not accidentally) spilling most of it down his yellow shorts, then bounds over to Mum. She gulps the water down.

'Got to say, I'm not feeling very relaxed so far,' says Clive.

'Oh, it's a shame to laugh at them,' hisses a woman behind me to her friend. 'They're so sincere and really believe what they're saying, which makes a nice change.'

**5.19 p.m.**
Incredibly, Mum and Dad leave to huge applause. Then Clive leaps in front of them. 'I'm going to try all the exercises you taught me. Honestly, I am,' he says, winking at the audience.

'That's excellent news.' Dad looks really chuffed.

Clive turns to the audience and winks again. 'How about if we invite our new friends' – he points to Mum and Dad – 'back next Monday. They can find out how I've got on with *mind* training. Would you like that?'

The audience start to cheer.

'Can you come back?' Clive asks my parents.

'I'm sure we can,' said Mum. 'We lead a very quiet life really.'

'Not for much longer though,' laughs Clive. 'Because you've cheered everyone up tonight, haven't you?'

The audience roar their agreement.

**5.40 p.m.**

Back in the green room, and Greta the Garden Guru is the first to congratulate Mum and Dad. 'You were so... so... unusual.' Then Mitchell speeds in to say the Twitter reaction to Mum and Dad has been 'overwhelming already'.

'Well, if it hadn't been for Louis,' says Dad, 'we'd be back home now.'

But Mitchell is already talking about a contact at breakfast television – and would Mum and Dad be interested in appearing on that too?

**6.55 p.m.**

We'd just arrived home, when there was a sharp tap on the front door. Mum and Dad actually jumped.

Mum hurtled out, then we heard her say, 'We might have guessed,' and laughing. Next, Elliot hurtled in, shouting to no one in particular, 'I never thought *Live at Five* would actually let my mum and dad on.'

'Thanks for that vote of confidence,' murmured Dad.

152

Accompanying Elliot were his friend Lee, and Lee's mum, Mrs Evans, who was saying to Mum and Dad, 'I've never known Clive invite guests back the very next week. You must be so proud.' Then she asked Mum, 'We were all wondering – did you actually have a coughing fit, or were you told to do that?'

'I'm afraid I really did,' said Mum. 'My throat just became incredibly dry.'

'Well, it all made for wonderful television,' said Mrs Evans. 'And knowing you were coughing authentically makes it even better.'

**7.25 p.m.**
Breakfast television have just confirmed they would like Mum and Dad to appear on Thursday morning.

'No stopping you both now,' said Mrs Evans.

Then Dad repeated that without me their nerves would have overwhelmed them tonight.

'So what did Louis actually do?' asked Mrs Evans.

'He gave us a mindfulness lesson,' smiled Dad, 'that we'll never forget.'

'And now,' shrieked Elliot, 'I'm living with superstars!'

\*     \*     \*

## Chapter Twenty
# Isla's Secret

**Tuesday May 6th**

**7.10 a.m.**
Woke up to find Mum and Dad standing over me.

'Are you awake, Louis?' hissed Mum.

'No,' I murmured. 'Call back in an hour when I won't be here.'

'We need to talk to you,' said Mum.

'Can you leave a message?'

But instead Dad asked, 'Last night on *Live at Five*, do you think people were laughing *at* us or *with* us?'

'We want you to be really honest now,' added

Mum.

I sat up in bed. Now, if I was telling the truth – well, the people around me were laughing and sniggering at them the whole time. But I couldn't tell Mum and Dad that and destroy all their confidence.

'What I think is...' I began. Mum and Dad actually leaned forward. No wonder I felt wise. 'OK, there might have been a tiny amount of sniggering, BUT people really enjoyed watching you too. You saw that by the way they clapped you at the end. And I heard a woman near me say how "sincere" you both were. And that you both "really believed" what you were saying.'

'That's very inspiring to hear,' said Dad. 'And you've given us something to think about. Thank you, Louis.'

I closed my eyes and threw myself under the covers once more. 'Will you see yourselves out?'

**4.03 p.m.**
When I came home, Mum and Dad were watching themselves on catch-up.

'Don't worry,' said Dad. 'All this attention isn't going to our heads. We're scrutinising ourselves very critically.'

'I believe you,' I grinned.

'No, we are,' insisted Mum, 'as we think we

could improve. Don't you, Louis?'

Yeah, MASSIVELY, I thought, but I only said, 'Well, maybe a bit.'

'But despite our mistakes,' said Mum, 'people do seem to have liked us.'

'They loved you,' I cried. 'Have you seen all those comments on Twitter?'

'We might have taken a quick peek,' admitted Mum.

'The trouble is,' said Dad, 'although we left the green room feeling relaxed, the moment we arrived on stage, all our inhibitions returned. Incredibly, people still responded to us. But they'll be so much more responsive once we've sorted out all our weaknesses.' His eyes glowed excitedly. 'We're taking today and tomorrow off as holiday from work to rehearse exactly what we want to say on breakfast television,' Dad chuckled. 'By Thursday, we'll have improved so much no one will believe it's us.'

## Wednesday May 7th

**4.15 p.m.**
Coming home from school, I heard someone whisper my name. I whirled round – and there was Isla.

She smiled at me very anxiously. 'I've been

hoping I'd bump into you one day soon – and yet really dreading it too, which I know sounds a bit confusing. But anyway, here you are.'

'That's what I am – here,' I agreed.

'Louis, I am so sorry,' she burst out, 'for pretending you were my boyfriend at Tiffany's party when you expressly asked me not to—'

'Forget it,' I interrupted.

'I can't.'

'Well, I can,' I replied. 'Anyway, how is Charlie?'

Isla made a face.

'But I thought you two were back together?' I said.

'Oh, he wanted to go out with me again, but he still wanted to see Tiffany as well.'

'Talk about greedy.'

'You know, Louis, before the party I'd really built Charlie up into something very special. But afterwards, when he sort of wanted to get back with me, I saw through him and thought, you're nothing special really.'

'And obviously very fickle,' I added.

'Exactly. But if I hadn't gone to that party, I'd still be imagining he was something he so isn't, so thank you, Louis, for disillusioning me. Oh, that doesn't sound right, does it?'

'No,' I grinned.

'But you know what I mean.'

'I do, and don't worry, Isla, you'll find someone else.'

'Actually,' she smiled, 'I have already.'

'Hey, that was quick,' I cried.

'He doesn't know yet. It's a total secret. I want to tell him.' She smiled coyly at me. 'Do you think I should tell him?'

A gasp escaped from my lips.

'Oh, don't worry, it's not you!' she said at once, letting out a guffaw. It was a big relief, although I wish Isla hadn't laughed quite so loudly at the very idea of it being me. 'I like you very much as a friendly neighbourhood superstar, but that's all,' she said. 'Do you remember a boy I met with you once?'

'No.'

'Oh, you do. Blond hair, good-looking. He was at Tiffany's party too.'

I gaped at her. 'You don't mean Edgar?'

'Yes,' she said. 'He was putting the litter back in the bins the correct way, and I thought that was such a caring, lovely thing to do.'

'You did?' I was still really shocked.

'He seems a quality person, and so different to most of the boys I know. You're his friend. So, can you tell me some more about him?'

'Well, he was born aged 40,' I began.

'Oh, that's not fair,' she said defensively.

'No. OK, he's a good kid. He's loyal and funny – often not intentionally – and, oh yeah, he's very big on hobbies.'

'Such as?'

'Well,' I considered, 'I know he collects stuff... coins, stamps, rocks—'

'Louis!' Isla interrupted excitedly. 'I collect rocks. In fact, I've built up quite a good collection.'

I stared at her for a moment. 'Leave everything to me,' I said.

**4.25 p.m.**
I decided I'd tell Maddy first that Edgar had a fan. How she'd laugh.

**4.40 p.m.**
Maddy didn't laugh at all.

After I rang her and relayed the merry news, she said, very coldly, 'So you've seen her again then?'

'Maddy, I was on my way home and Isla called my name. What do you expect me to do, run for my life?'

Maddy sighed heavily down the phone. 'That girl! She's with one boy, then she moves on to you, now she's after Edgar.'

'Now just hold on there, Maddy.' I was getting

160

more than a bit annoyed now. 'Isla is a fan of mine – a big fan, you might even say. And stars are supposed to help out their fans. Not to mention has-beens.'

'You're not a has-been,' said Maddy quickly.

'But I can tell you, Isla is definitely not interested in me as a boyfriend—'

'You asked her then?' interrupted Maddy.

'What? Yes. No. You're confusing me now!'

'And how do you even know,' cried Maddy, 'that Edgar wants to see this girl?'

'I don't.'

There was a pause.

'Listen, Louis, don't do anything yet – I need to investigate this.'

'Investigate?' I echoed in disbelief. 'What are you going to do? Take Isla's fingerprints and—'

'Bye, Louis,' interrupted Maddy, and she rang off.

## Thursday May 8th

### 6.10 a.m.
The moment breakfast television starts, Elliot is sitting in front of the screen. He wants to be ready for Mum and Dad. Even though they aren't due for nearly two hours, and have, in fact, only just left for the studio.

161

**8.15 a.m.**

So there I was, slurping down cereal, while Mum and Dad were beamed onto my television. Not often you can write that. In fact, I've never been able to write it before. It was dead weird – but mostly in a good way. Especially as my parents were better – I might even say much better – than they were on *Live at Five*.

They weren't in their ghastly clothes for a start. When the presenter asked why, Mum and Dad said, 'I think we've demonstrated how unimportant appearance is. So we're ready to move on.' Now they were dressed exactly as if they were off to work and, as a result, looked tons better. They'd lost their flat deadpan voices too and sounded more like themselves. And all that rehearsing had certainly paid off, as they didn't dry up in the middle of a sentence once. In fact, they seemed almost normal, not like my usual embarrassing relics!

Only Elliot was disappointed. 'They didn't make me laugh once. They should have stuck on those weird clothes again.'

**8.30 a.m.**

On my way to school when Dad rang. 'We're coming home on a cloud of euphoria,' said Dad.

'Not bothering with the car then,' I quipped.

'We cracked it, didn't we?' said Dad proudly.

'It was as if you'd been droning away on TV for years.'

'Well, we were petrified before we went on,' said Dad, 'but as soon as we started, the nerves just fell away. We workshopped everything we wanted to say.'

'I didn't know you had a workshop,' I said.

'That's a media term, Louis – people use it when they're throwing ideas around,' said Dad airily. 'So we workshopped seven bullet points and remembered every one of them. We're going to workshop our return to *Live at Five* on Monday too. I really think we're on a roll now.'

**4.30 p.m.**
Now I am very confused.

You know I told you that my parents were vastly better on breakfast television – well, trust me, they really were. Only I've just been perusing their latest online comments and I can't believe it.

Here's a quick sample: '*I loved them when they were just being themselves, but now I can tell they want to be on television – and all their fun has vanished.*' And one more: '*Oh dear, they've lost all their innocence and are just not fresh and funny any more. Even their clothes are*

163

*boring now.'*

So basically, all these so-called adults agree with Elliot.

And he's seven and a half years old.

## Friday May 9th

### 4.43 p.m.
The good news is that my school has an inset day on Monday – the even better news is that Maddy's torture chamber is closed too, and Mum has just suggested Maddy might like to accompany us to *Live at Five* and look 'behind the scenes'. I really think fame is improving Mum's character. She never used to come up with such awesome ideas.

### 5.12 p.m.
There are some things in life you think you will NEVER, ever see and I've just seen one of them.

I was about to ring Maddy's doorbell when the door opened so suddenly I nearly fell backwards.

And then I saw who was standing on the doorstep and nearly fell over again.

It was Isla.

## Chapter Twenty-One

# Maddy's Incredible Idea

'Hi, Louis,' said Isla. I could only goggle at her. 'And bye, Louis,' she said, grinning broadly at Maddy standing behind her. With that, she strolled away.

'That was Isla.' My words came out in a strangled squawk. 'And she was here in your house,' I added, just in case Maddy hadn't noticed.

'Well, I thought it was time I met her,' said Maddy. 'Especially as Edgar's much more sensitive than he looks. And I really didn't want him hurt. And he needs someone to look out for him and that's me, because...' She hesitated.

'Because that's what you do,' I said. 'You look

out for him – and me.'

Maddy nodded. 'Exactly. Anyway, now I've met her, I've decided it's all right, and you can tell Edgar that Isla likes him.'

'Got your permission, have I?'

'And I think you should tell Edgar right away.'

'Sure you don't want to come with me? You can check I say it in the right way.'

Maddy took me seriously and considered for a moment before saying, 'No, I think it's better if it's just the two of you.'

'OK, well before I leave for my match-making mission, would you like to come to *Live at Five* on Monday? Mum and Dad are back on it by popular demand and they wondered—'

'I'd love to,' interrupted Maddy. 'And let me know how you get on with Edgar, won't you? Bye, Louis.'

'Hey, wait a second,' I said. 'So what did you and Isla talk about then?'

'Edgar, mainly,' said Maddy.

'Right, OK.' I still hovered. 'But are we all right now? And you're not really planning to take a break from me soon, are you? Answer the last question first.'

A small smile flashed across Maddy's face, but she didn't answer any of my questions. Instead she said again, 'Bye, Louis,' and firmly closed the door.

Women.

**5.48 p.m.**

When I dropped round to Edgar's house he was in his bedroom reading a book about killer whales. 'I felt like some light reading,' Edgar explained. 'This is a surprise,' he added.

'Isn't it. But I have some news for you about Isla – you remember her?'

'Most certainly.'

'Well, she'd like to inspect your collection of rocks some time.'

'I don't understand,' he said.

'Well, amazingly Isla collects rocks too. I thought you were the only one in the known universe. But no, it seems there are two of you. Isla also said she thought you were quite good-looking. I was absolutely certain that she'd mixed you up with someone else. But no, incredibly, it really was you she meant. So how about it?'

Edgar was now sitting bolt upright in his chair. But he didn't say a word. 'Have your batteries run out?' I enquired.

He looked up. 'I'm flabbergasted.'

'I can understand that,' I grinned. 'And she's not even short-sighted – at least, I don't think she is.'

'I had noticed Isla,' he went on. 'She is very pretty, but I wasn't at all sure what to do about it. Especially as... well, at my old school I was the boy who always stood on his own at the edge of the playground. No one ever really spoke to me. They'd decided I was zero fun.'

'How unfair,' I declared. 'You're a tiny bit fun. Occasionally.'

Edgar gave a short laugh, rather like a burp. 'May I ask what would you do if you weren't you but were, in fact, me?'

'What a truly horrible thought... but I'd invite Isla round, definitely.'

He thought for a moment. 'I do also have a drawer full of badges and I am adept at a large number of board games.'

'Edgar,' I said, 'she'll never want to leave.'

## Saturday May 10th

I wandered into the kitchen and heard Dad saying, 'What an insult, calling us a big yawn,' then laughing in a very fake way. He and Mum were looking at their latest online comments.

'Have you seen these, Louis?' asked Mum.

'I might have glanced at them, but there are some good ones in there too.'

'Where?' demanded Mum.

'Oh, they're about,' I said vaguely. 'And it's good to get some bad comments too, as it gets more people talking about you.'

'Well, we should certainly start some conversations going then,' said Dad. 'I really didn't think we were dull.' He gave that false laugh again. 'Are we boring, Louis?' Dad demanded suddenly.

Of course he and Mum were. And I meant that as a compliment. After all, no kid wants crazy parents rushing about and being zany all the time. The best parents leave all the fun stuff to us.

But this wasn't the moment to explain that. So I just said, 'Look, I bet there are people all over the country breathing from their diaphragm, who would never have thought of doing that if it hadn't been for you. And to those people on Twitter who said you were boring and dull, I say, just wait until they see you on TV next Monday!'

I know how to cheer people up.

## Sunday May 11th

**11.05 a.m.**
Rang Edgar, keen to know how his evening with Isla (he refuses to call it a date) went. 'Quite

pleasing,' was all he would say, which was a bit of a let-down. But maybe he didn't need to say anything else as he sounded dead happy. And guess what – he is off to view Isla's rock collection TONIGHT.

**11.20 a.m.**
Called Maddy and said, 'Greetings, my name is Wilhelm and you have been chosen to take part in an international survey. You only need to answer one vital question. All right?'

'Take it away, Wilhelm,' said Maddy.

'Are you still taking a break from that well-known comedian – well known in his own bedroom, anyway – Louis the Laugh? Take your time – but answer immediately…'

Maddy said softly, 'I shall be delaying our break again.'

'Only delaying!'

'If you'd let me finish, Wilhelm,' said Maddy, 'I shall be delaying my break from Louis the Laugh – permanently.'

After that, my feelings were so strong, I could only yell deafeningly down the phone, '*YEEEEEES*,' before adding, 'You have made me, Wilhelm, and Louis very happy.'

\*   \*   \*

170

## Monday May 12th

**11.00 a.m.**
It's 'Return to *Live at Five* Day' and I've just heard Mum on the phone saying, 'That is out of the question too. I will ask my husband, but I'm sure he will agree with me. I'm very sorry, Nina. Goodbye.' Then Mum put the phone down and spotted me.

'If you thought I was eavesdropping,' I said, 'you'd be quite right.'

'That was Nina,' explained Mum, 'from *Live at Five*.' Well, I'd guessed that much...

'So what terrible thing did she want you to do?' I asked.

'Wear the clothes we wore last Monday – or something equally wacky. I tried to explain that we're not about dressing up. So why should we have to resort to silly gimmicks?'

'Anything else?'

Mum sighed. 'Nina thinks your dad and I should deliberately make some mistakes when we're on the show.'

'But why?'

'Nina said it would help us become authentic again. But I didn't know we'd stopped being authentic.'

**2.40 p.m.**

Mum and Dad have not dressed up – they are in their normal casual clothes. And the car is due any minute. So next time I write will be from the green room.

More soon.

**9.30 p.m.**

I know. I know.

I'd promised to write to you long before this.

But I have got a good reason!

Get ready for— Actually, no. I'm not going to even give you a clue. Sorry and all that, but I want you to be as totally amazed as me by what's happened tonight.

It began in the green room. Mitchell strode in with Nina trailing behind him. He was smiling as usual, but he seemed especially purposeful too. And he spoke to Mum and Dad very quickly, as if he wanted to get this conversation over as speedily as possible.

'Apologies, guys,' he said, 'but it's an absolutely packed show so although Clive will talk to you at the start as before, he will only be able to let you talk very briefly about mindfulness. And then ask you only one question – namely: 'What has been your highlight of the past week?' If you could have a very short answer ready that would be perfect. And then... you'll be free to go home. We'll have a car ready for you, of course.'

So, Mum and Dad's appearance this time was going to be of the 'if you blink, you'll miss it' variety. It had hardly been worth them coming all this way for that. And why had their time been cut so short? Was it really because it was a busy show? Or had the producers read Mum and Dad's latest online comments and decided they just weren't hot on the internet any more?

But my parents took it remarkably well. I felt sort of proud of them actually. 'We only appeared last week,' said Dad. 'So we don't want to be greedy.' But he was very disappointed, I could tell.

'Thanks for your understanding.' Mitchell sounded relieved. He added confidingly, 'Every day here is busy, but it's especially chaotic today. And now, at the very last minute we heard that Jasper – our warm-up comedian – is unwell. Of course, it's too late to get a replacement. So I shall have to try to entertain them somehow with—'

'Louis can stand in for Jasper,' cut in Maddy suddenly.

Mitchell was confused. 'Err, who's Louis?'

'That's Louis.' Maddy pointed right at me.

Mitchell immediately shook his head. 'They're

a nice audience but they like Jasper a lot. So they might give his replacement a difficult time.'

'That won't bother Louis at all.' Maddy was brimming with confidence. 'He's performed in front of audiences much tougher than this; he's been a regular on Noah and Lily. And anyway, I think they will be fascinated to see the son of your first two guests.'

Maddy nodded at me to stand up. I did so, grinning, and said, 'She's my agent, as if you hadn't already guessed.'

Mitchell, still looking highly doubtful, said half to himself, 'I suppose his age will make him a novelty.' He turned to Mum and Dad. 'What do you think?'

They glanced at each other before Mum said quietly, 'I think Louis will entertain your audience all right. He certainly knows a lot of jokes.'

'Well,' Mitchell wavered, 'we haven't got—' I'm certain he was about to say 'anyone else', but at the last moment he tactfully changed it to 'very much time'.

And before I knew it, there I was, standing in the wings, having a very small microphone clipped onto my jacket. 'We will look after you,' whispered Nina. 'And Mitchell will stay on stage with you and be ready to step in whenever you

174

wish.' It was clear she wasn't at all certain I'd be any good.

Meanwhile, Mitchell was telling the audience that Jasper couldn't do the warm-up tonight. There were loud groans at this news. He was extremely popular, all right. Was I really going to stroll out there now and make up for their disappointment? Well, I'd have to make sure I began strongly by telling...

I froze.

My face went hot.

I'd forgotten every joke I'd ever known.

## Chapter Twenty-Two

# 'Om' to the Rescue

One moment I'd known thousands of jokes; the very next they'd all vanished from my memory.

Meanwhile, Mitchell was saying, 'So now I want you all to give a big hand to a talented new young comedian called... *Louis.*'

Nina gave me a gentle nudge. 'Louis, you're on,' she hissed.

But I had crumpled like a wet sock and couldn't move or speak – let alone tell a joke.

It had happened to me once before, when I ventured into Marcus Capel's hotel room. A spot of emergency aid for his son had restored my confidence and memory then – but this time... I was all alone!

'Louis, you're on,' repeated Nina, looking so anxious I wouldn't have been surprised if she needed some emergency aid soon.

I watched her signal to Mitchell that there was a delay and heard him say, 'Louis will be on very shortly – but while we're waiting, let me tell you about some highlights on the show next week.'

The minutes were ticking by. Soon, it would be too late. My chance was slipping away forever.

If only I could RELAX.

That's what I had to do. But why does telling yourself to relax always have completely the opposite effect?

Now I was tenser than ever.

And nothing could save me now.

'*Om.*'

That silly word just floated into my head. But I whispered it, saying *Ommmm* (not *Um*), and letting the sound vibrate through my whole body, exactly as Mum and Dad had taught me.

'*Ommmm*,' I said again. And then, almost without realising it, I started closing my eyes and doing the deep breathing routine too – breathing in, holding my breath for a few seconds, then breathing out again.

And I felt different somehow.

Much calmer, for a start.

Then jokes began flashing back into my head at an incredible rate. It was truly amazing. And all due to the power of *Om*. But that would mean my parents were actually right about something – which was just too incredible to believe.

For luck though, I said *Ommmm* loudly and jubilantly one last time.

Nina leaped as though she had been stung. 'What did you say?' she quavered.

'Just *Ommmm*,' I replied.

'Louis,' asked Nina anxiously, 'would you like me to take you back to the green room?'

I smiled serenely at her. 'Why on earth would you want to do that? Let's go, shall we?'

With doubt oozing from every pore, she gave Mitchell the signal. He announced me again and I strolled onto that stage to decidedly scattered applause. No one was at all excited or even pleased to see me. No wonder Mitchell stood right beside me, as if we were a double act. He was all ready to get me off stage dead fast.

'Let's give Louis a chance, shall we? He is very young and has never done anything like this before.' Mitchell was pleading with the audience.

The very next moment I was off, performing an act I'd practised so many times in my bedroom.

'Hey, guess what, I'm one of the world's

leading experts on animals. No, really. Anything you want to know about the natural world, I can tell you. For instance, where do sheep go in their holidays? *The Baa-hamas.*

'Why do birds fly south in the winter? *Because it's too far to walk.*

'What goes zzub zzub? *A bee flying backwards.*

'You're learning so much about nature, aren't you?' I grinned round at them.

And that's when something incredible happened. Not only did people start laughing, but a buzz ran through the audience too as people murmured, 'That boy with the biggest ears known to humanity isn't too bad.'

I was starting to win them over.

Well, there was no stopping me then. The laughs started to get louder and then, quite unexpectedly, a huge laugh – like a great wave – erupted all around the room.

That sound was so intoxicating, I felt... weightless. In fact, if I'd suddenly soared up into the air, I wouldn't have been at all surprised.

Before I knew it, Mitchell – who had returned to the back of the stage – was coming forward again and saying, 'Thank you very much, Louis.' But only the first couple of rows heard him. There was too much noise with people clapping and stamping their feet.

'That was good work,' Mitchell murmured to me. He sounded totally astonished. Then he steered me over to Nina, who guided me down to the front row. People continued applauding me and some even leaned forward to pat me on the shoulder as I jumped down next to Maddy.

Now Mitchell was saying, 'Thank you, everyone,' but the audience still went on clapping. In the end, he had to put his hand up like a teacher in assembly. 'Thank you, everyone!' he shouted again.

Maddy and I exchanged dazed smiles and she squeezed my hand tightly, while Mitchell finally managed to calm the audience down and declared, 'We are now going *Live at Five!*'

Clive strolled onto the stage and introduced Mum and Dad again. There were disappointed sighs as the audience realised Mum and Dad weren't in costume this time.

Then Dad explained how to do an early-morning breathing exercise. His voice was still a bit flat, but he didn't make one mistake and I thought he went through it very well. But the audience were already beginning to get restless.

Clive, sensing the audience's impatience, cut Dad short by saying, 'Well, that sounds like a lot of fun,' and winking at everyone as he said it. 'Now, I've got to ask you both to tell me,

BRIEFLY, what's been your highlight of your past week?'

Mum looked at Dad before saying, 'I think we're in agreement on this one.'

'We really are,' said Dad.

'The suspense is unbearable,' grinned Clive through his leathery face. 'So come on, was it meeting me?'

'Afraid not,' beamed Dad. 'It was watching our son on this very stage, just a few minutes ago.'

## Chapter Twenty-Three

# Making 200 New Friends

'You see,' Mum went on, 'we've been trying to stop Louis wasting his time on comedy. We thought it was distracting him from finding his true self. But right in front of our eyes, we've seen that comedy is a true and wonderful part of who he really is.'

'So we think' – Dad's voice was suddenly very loud – 'that everyone should see more of Louis's comedy act. RIGHT NOW.' He peered into the audience. 'What do you all think?'

Well, the room just erupted and the very next thing I knew, Dad was urging me up onto the stage. 'This is it, Louis,' whispered Maddy. 'Your chance at last. The chance you **so** deserve!' I took a slow, deep breath, while my heart turned a double somersault.

And then Nina was helping me up on stage again, while Mum, Dad and what sounded like the entire audience cheered. Meanwhile, Clive was lumbering about the stage like a confused bear. I wondered what he was going to say.

Would he tell me to take a bow and then go and sit down again? But instead he pushed his face right up to mine – up close he looked deeply, weirdly orange, and I wasn't wild about his breath either – before bellowing down my ear, 'Look what chaos you've caused, young man. But on a live show ANYTHING can happen – and right now, I really think it's been taken over. And we have no choice but to hear...' He paused.

'Louis,' prompted Mum.

'Louis the Laugh,' added Dad.

'Well, come on, Louis the Laugh!' yelled Clive. *Make us laugh!'*

Nina sped forward to quickly attach a tiny microphone onto my jacket again – and there I was under the glow of the TV lights, thinking, after all that build-up, wouldn't it be terrible if I turned out to be rubbish now? But I quickly swatted that thought away and said, 'It's awesome to be back with you all.' And right away the audience began clapping. Before I'd even uttered one joke.

I tell you, that applause was such a shock it took my breath away for a moment. I actually gulped. But then I was off.

'Just before I came on, I was reading a book – *The History of Glue. Couldn't put it down.*

'Do you know what the king said when he went to the dentist? "*I've come for my crown.*"'

I grinned at the audience. 'Ah, you like that one? Well, you know, I told jokes at the zoo once. *Got babooned off.*'

They laughed at EVERY single joke. But do you know what was even more amazing? I wasn't scared. Not even nervous. Instead, it felt as if I'd made a bunch of brand-new friends – 200 new friends, in fact – and I was having the time of my life telling them all jokes.

And I completely forgot my act was being broadcast on television. Suppose my parents would say I was 'living in the moment'. Anyway, Clive let me go on much longer than I'd expected. And in the end, he only stopped me because they had to go to a commercial break.

The very next thing I remember was Mum, Dad, Maddy and me having this jubilant group hug in the middle of the green room. We were like a band of football supporters whose team had just won a final 20–nil. No wonder we all had big silly grins stuck onto our faces.

Finally, looking right at Mum and Dad, I said, 'What you have done today is the finest thing parents could ever do for their kids. You gave up appearing on television for me. Thank you.'

'Best decision we ever made,' said Dad, 'and actually, your mum and I had already decided it was time to fold up our tents and steal away. Tonight was to be our farewell performance—'

He was interrupted by Mitchell tearing in and saying, 'A big thank-you for your involvement today. You were absolutely great. And your car will be here very shortly.'

You sensed he had said this many times before and he was about to dart away again when Maddy sprang forward. 'You will need this,' she said. 'My contact details, as Louis's agent.' And she gave Mitchell her card very solemnly, as if she were giving him a valuable treasure map or something.

Mitchell glanced at the card for a moment, and then nodded as if remembering something. Then he looked up at me. 'Clive was very pleased with your contribution and he wanted to let you know that.'

We waited for Mitchell to go on and say: 'In fact, Clive was so pleased he wants you to be on the show next Monday, as well. And every

Monday from now on.'

It would have been so incredible if Mitchell had said that. But he didn't. Never uttered another word before disappearing, in fact.

But you know what, it doesn't matter. I mean, I've just had the best moment of my life tonight. A moment I couldn't have predicted happening even a few hours ago. And Mum, Dad – and Maddy – were here with me. What more could I want?

It's just a shame I'm at the end of another diary. Still, I can't think of a better moment to bow low and say GOODB—

No, stop!

Please don't put my diary down yet, because you will miss hearing about...

THE REAL
MARCUS CAPEL

CONTRACT

# Extra! Extra!

## Saturday May 17th

What I so want to tell you about started two evenings ago.

Maddy came round and the conversation went like this:

MADDY: I've just been talking to Marcus Capel.

ME: Oh yeah, he wants me to perform at his son Mason's birthday party next month. What day in June is it?

MADDY: Haven't a clue.

ME: What did you talk about then?

MADDY: Louis, it wasn't that Marcus Capel.

ME: How many are there?

MADDY: (voice rising) This was the one we

thought we'd met but hadn't. Only now I have – well, I've not met him yet, but I have spoken to him.

ME: Now I'm very confused.

MADDY: (practically shouting now) Marcus Capel, the real one, got my contact details from Mitchell and he wants to see you on Saturday afternoon!

ME: (speaking very, very slowly) Not to audition for *Make Me Laugh*?

MADDY: No, to have a look at your maths homework. Of course, that's what he wants you to do… your own special, private audition too, at a studio, only about ten miles away where he has an office.

As I said, that was two days ago – now I have just returned from meeting Marcus Capel.

Mum, Dad and, of course, Maddy went with me. (Elliot was outraged he couldn't join us too – and was packed off to Nan and Grandad's instead.)

And when we reached the studio I said to Maddy, 'Can you believe that inside this building right now, Marcus Capel is waiting to audition me?'

'You haven't even got to pretend you're the hotel comedian this time,' smiled Maddy.

'Remember?'

'I'll never forget that afternoon at the Belle Vue.' I grinned. 'Hey, do you think I should ask this Marcus Capel for some ID – just to prove he is the genuine article?'

As we went up in the lift, I started imagining Marcus Capel's office. It'd be vast, of course, and he'd be reclining in a red leather chair which swung wildly about. (I'd love a chair like that.)

But in fact, his office was smallish and deeply ordinary. There was no sign of a red leather chair, or indeed of Marcus Capel. Even Mum and Dad looked a bit apprehensive.

'So... where is he?' asked Dad. And just like that, in he walked.

The real Marcus Capel.

He was a tall, thin, middle-aged man in a blue suit, with a surprisingly quiet voice and very bright eyes. A smallish, sun-tanned man with springy yellow hair, called Bruce, accompanied him, and it was Bruce who arranged the chairs in a semi-circle.

We were all just sitting down together when, would you believe it, someone's mobile went off.

What total idiot hadn't switched off their phone? I bet it was Dad. He'd never mastered modern technology. Dad thought it was his phone too and began rooting about in his bag,

189

muttering apologies and going bright red.

'Can't take him anywhere,' I said to Marcus Capel. 'But you've got to remember, when Dad was growing up mobile phones hadn't been invented – or they were so huge you had to be a heavyweight champion to lift one.'

Then quite suddenly I realised, the total idiot wasn't Dad and was, of course, ME. So then I was the one fumbling about in my pocket and getting all tense, especially as Bruce was looking a bit impatient.

'It's only Hollywood,' I quipped. 'They can call back.'

Marcus Capel actually laughed then (Bruce sort of did too).

And then, to Maddy's and my huge surprise, Marcus Capel didn't ask me to tell him a single joke. (I'd only prepared a gazillion of them.) Instead, he said he'd just like to ask me a few questions.

I wondered if they'd be the sort of questions Noah and Lily were always answering. Vital ones like, 'If you were a biscuit, what sort of biscuit would you be?'

Well, I was prepared for that one.

I'd be a chocolate Hobnob, of course.

But instead he asked me about appearing on *Live at Five*, which he and 'his team' had all watched several times, apparently. He seemed keenly interested in all the background details I gave him.

Then Marcus Capel leaned back in his grey chair and said, 'Louis, in one sentence describe you to me. Tell me anything you like.'

Quick as a flash I replied, 'I'm a person who loves to laugh whatever the reason – and make you laugh too.'

He nodded (he'd done a lot of nodding when I was talking, which I supposed was a good sign) and I waited for my next question. Instead he very casually mentioned that they were looking for someone the same age as the contestants to co-host *Make Me Laugh*. 'This person will chat to the contestants and help put them at their ease; would you be at all interested in doing this, Louis?'

My first thought was: What a shame this is only a dream. Still, the quality of my dreams was definitely improving.

Then I heard Mum and Dad droning on that they needed to know how much of my time this would take, as I had important exams coming up. But I would never allow such tedious dialogue into any dream of mine. So this had to be really happening.

I quickly piped up, 'I'll go to night school if I

have to – but it's a big fat yes from me. I'll do it. Definitely. Do you want me to sign somewhere or give you my thumbprint?'

Maddy laughed, but Mum and Dad continued to look like a right pair of misery guts.

Marcus Capel carefully explained to Mum and Dad that the schedule would be arranged so that it didn't take up too much of my time. Also, it would be only seven shows – one a week. Plus the Grand Final, of course.

Suddenly Marcus Capel stood up. He said he thought I had exactly the right personality and attitude to co-host *Make me Laugh*, but he would leave us to talk about it, as he realised it was an important decision.

He and Bruce closed the door behind them, leaving Maddy and me sternly eyeballing my parents.

'Louis, we do know how much you want this—' Mum began.

'Great, so let's get signing that contract.'

'I have two pens right here,' added Maddy.

'What an agent,' I said. 'You've got two pens just in case one runs out, haven't you?'

'Of course,' said Maddy. 'In fact, I nearly brought three.'

'Louis,' said Mum, frowning a little, 'nothing you want is ever given away free, you know.

Along the way there will be sacrifices and setbacks and disappointments too.'

'That's right, cheer us all up,' I said.

'No, we're keeping your feet on the ground,' said Dad. 'It's tricky being in the world of show business. And we know a bit about it now after our half-second of fame.'

'But what are you both saying?' I asked, positively bursting with impatience now.

Mum suddenly looked right at me, her face spreading into a huge smile. 'We had to check everything first, but of course it's a Yes.'

Maddy and I immediately started leaping about very excitedly.

'Hey, calm down, both of you,' urged Mum, 'or they will wonder what's going on in here. We hope you do know how pleased your dad and I are about this.'

'And so proud of you, Louis,' Dad said hoarsely. 'Now, before they come back in, was there anything else you wanted to ask us?'

I nodded solemnly. 'There was, actually.' I paused. 'But I don't quite know how to put it.'

'Say whatever you want,' murmured Mum, both her and Dad looking concerned now.

I said slowly, 'Will you both promise me that you'll never in the whole of your life... wear those ridiculous clothes **ever** again?'

'What a cheek,' said Dad, a grin immediately spreading right across his face. Then he started laughing. Everyone did. We were all still laughing when Marcus Capel came back into his office.

'Now that's a good sound,' he said.

I grinned up at him. 'I'd say it's the best sound in the whole world.'

That's why I'd like to leave you laughing too.

Here's a very silly joke – just for you:

What's black and white and green? *A zebra with a runny nose.*

Smile on!

Your friend,
Louis the Laugh

# The Great How to Change Your Parents into Superstars Quiz!

1  **How does Maddy help Louis get past the security man at the Belle Vue hotel?**
   a) She rushes in and shouts, 'Fire Fire!' at the top of her voice.
   b) She coughs loudly and says she's about to faint.
   c) She pretends she is staying at the hotel and has lost her key.

2  **Isla and Louis observe Edgar behaving 'very strangely'. What is he doing?**
   a) Taking rubbish out of the bin and putting it straight back in again.

b) Standing by the bin and telling people the correct way to deposit their rubbish.

c) Reciting a poem in the street about the need to clean up our environment.

**3 What is the name of the internet show that comes to Louis's house?**
a) *Stars of Tomorrow*
b) *Dare to Be Different*
c) *My Struggle*

**4 At the end of the mindfulness morning, what challenge does Steve set the adults?**
a) Tell their neighbours all about mindfulness.
b) Do deep breathing every morning for half an hour.
c) Turn up for the drop-in session in their 'fun' clothes.

**5 At the mindfulness morning, Steve introduces his 'buddy', who will teach everyone how to breathe. What is her name?**
a) Maria
b) Marianne
c) Marta

**6** At Tiffany's party where does Louis hide?
a) Behind the sofa.
b) In the bathroom.
c) Underneath all the coats.

**7** Why doesn't Maddy spend the weekend at her aunt's house as planned?
a) Her aunt had a bad cold.
b) The pipes in her aunt's house had burst.
c) Her aunt is going on a surprise holiday.

**8** What is the name of the TV show on which both Louis's parents and Louis appear?
a) *The Five O'Clock Show*
b) *In Town Tonight*
c) *Live at Five*

**9** Which hobby do Isla and Edgar share?
a) They both collect rocks.
b) They both collect coins.
c) They both collect stamps.

**10** Who does Louis finally meet at the end of the book?
a) Marcus Townsend
b) Marcus Capel
c) Mark Wallace

If you scored **8 or above**...

# OUTSTANDING!

You know more about
Louis's life than
he does.

If you scored
**6 or 7**...

# VERY GOOD!

You are a true
Louis fan!

If you scored
**5 or less**...

# GOOD!

Why not read the
book again and
have another go!

WANTED!

# Pete Johnson...

## ...answers your questions about Louis, writing and being funny

**How much is Louis like you?**

Well, we both certainly love comedy – and making people laugh. And I agree with Louis that laughter is the best sound in the world.

But he is far braver than me. I would never dare to be a stand-up comedian. I'd be too scared no one would smile, let alone laugh.

So I am a bit like Louis – but Maddy too. And Edgar. And yes, Louis's parents! In fact, there's something of me in every one of the main characters.

**Why do you think the Louis books are so popular?**

Well, first of all I'm thrilled they are – and around the world too! But the truth is, I don't really know. Readers do tell me that whenever they feel fed-up or a bit miserable, they turn to a Louis book to cheer themselves up. And they see Louis as their friend. So maybe that's a clue. I'm really proud Louis lifts people's spirits.

**What are the questions you are asked the most about the Louis books?**

Who is Louis really? Can I meet him? Where exactly does he live? Do you have his address? People are so disappointed when I tell them Louis only lives inside my head. The great thing is, he now lives in their heads too.

**Is it hard writing comedy?**

Yes, especially at eight o'clock in the morning when I don't feel awake, let alone remotely funny. The secret is, never try to be amusing, as that can make your writing seem very forced. Instead, describe what is happening and how the characters are feeling – and make it as real as possible – and hopefully the humour will bubble up out of the situations.

## Do parents read your books?

Yes, they do – and I'm relieved to tell you they laugh as well. The book they talk about the most is *My Parents Are Driving Me Crazy*. They like the way that, in amongst all the comedy, I also write about how lost and lonely Louis's dad feels when he suddenly loses his job.

## Louis is a big fan of P.G. Wodehouse. Are you too?

I certainly am. P.G. Wodehouse is, in fact, my comedy hero. He wrote many books and I believe I have every one of them. I also keep a signed copy of one of his titles in my study to inspire and encourage me!

## What are the best and worst things about being a writer?

For me, the worst thing is starting a new book. I just stare at all those blank pages and gulp – a lot. I can't tell you how incredibly nervous I become. It is as if it's my first day at school.

The best things are those very special occasions when it doesn't feel like doing work at all – the characters completely take over and all I have to do is write down, as quickly as I can, everything they are telling me. It is the most exhilarating and exciting feeling.

Something else that is great – not having to leave my house in the morning and wait in the rain, on a crowded platform, for a train which is always late (like several of my friends do)! Instead, I merely stroll into my study with a mug of tea and a chocolate biscuit – and vanish into the world of my imagination.

If you enjoyed this book,
why not discover more of
**Louis's hilarious adventures**
with this sample from...

ISBN 978-1-78270-160-6

# Chapter One
# Dad Acts Like a Big Poo

**Monday November 18th**

**4.30 p.m.**
My bedroom walls have been invaded – by Post-it Notes. Dead rude stuff too, like …

LOUIS, WHY SHOULD I MAKE YOUR BED TODAY? HOW LONG WOULD IT TAKE YOU TO DO IT?

LOUIS, DON'T LEAVE ALL THAT MESS ON THE FLOOR FOR ME TO CLEAN UP, DO IT YOURSELF.

LOUIS, ALWAYS TAKE YOUR MUGS DOWNSTAIRS.

DON'T JUST LEAVE THEM ON THE WINDOW
SILL FOR ME TO DEAL WITH.

'Dad's done exactly the same in my room,' wailed
Elliot, my midget brother. 'So it's like it's not my
bedroom any more.'

Now Mum had often dropped into my bedroom
to do a spot of cleaning. And I'd never minded.
In fact, I was happy to let her tidy up my room
whenever she wished.

But then Dad lost his job and Mum was
offered a full-time post at the estate agents. So
they decided to do a swap.

This is Dad's very first day as a stay-at-home
dad. Well, he's got off to a truly terrible start.
Can you believe he didn't even bother to carry
my dirty mugs downstairs? Talk about lazy.
He'd just grumped about, bunging up snotty
notes everywhere.

'When I saw my bedroom, I was so mad,' said
Elliot, 'I marched downstairs and shouted, "Dad,
you're acting like a big poo!"'

'You didn't?'

'Well, I wanted to, but I thought I'd wait for
you.'

I nodded and said, 'It can't be healthy for our
impressionable young minds to be exposed to all
this bossiness. Really, Dad's very lucky I didn't

call *Childline*. But he has to be stopped: and he will be – after I've cleared up my room.'

Elliot looked shocked.

'No, the Post-it Notes must be obeyed.' Then in one mighty movement I picked up the mountains of stuff on the floor and hurled it all under my bed. Elliot giggled. Next I dashed about ripping down every one of Dad's notes and threw them under the bed too.

Elliot was falling about laughing now.

'Right, now for Dad,' I said.

'Yeah, let's sort him out,' said Elliot eagerly.

We marched downstairs together.

Dad was hoovering in a revoltingly, enthusiastic way, really ramming the hoover into every corner. But when he saw us he switched the hoover off and said, 'Hoovering is more tiring than it looks, you know. Good fun, though. So how's everything going?'

'Very badly,' I said. And Elliot and I stood grave-faced either side of him.

'Now, what can be wrong?' said Dad, grinning away. He'd been in a wildly, cheerful mood since first thing this morning when he'd gone on and on about how lucky he was to be escaping the daily grind. I hated to burst his bubble. But things had to be said.

'How would you like it, Dad,' I asked, 'if I

stuck up notes all over your bedroom?'

'But I'm not asking you to clean *my* bedroom,' he replied. 'And I only put up a few friendly suggestions ...'

'Friendly...?' Elliot and I echoed disbelievingly.

'I just wondered, boys,' said Dad, 'if you'd like to make more of a contribution to cleaning your rooms.'

I considered for a second. 'No, we wouldn't.'

'Ah, but this is where it gets interesting,' he said.

'I doubt that,' I muttered.

'Up to now, you haven't had the right kit.'

'Dad, we're not in the army,' I said.

'But now you have.' That's when he handed us both giant green dusters, the size of pillowcases. 'These are your very own dusters to keep,' he beamed.

'Really,' I muttered.

'Oh yes, I went out and got them for you specially.'

Some dads shower their sons with computer games, comics and tickets for football games – my dad buys us dusters.

'So, nothing to stop you getting stuck in now,' he grinned.

'Mum never asked us to do any dusting,' said Elliot.

'But now your mum has joined the full-time workforce, so I'm in charge of the house – and I will be doing things a little differently to her. And I've decided that keeping your bedrooms clean and tidy will be your own personal responsibility. However, I shall always be available to help and advise you.'

'You're spoiling us,' I muttered.

'I think we're going to make a great team,' he said.

After he charged back to his hoovering, Elliot glared down at the unfamiliar object in his hand. 'What are we going to do with this?'

'Lose it as soon as possible. Don't worry, he'll have forgotten all about it in a couple of days,' I said.

**7.05 p.m.**

Normally Dad would stagger home about six o'clock and then sink down on the sofa, the laptop balanced on his knees, still doing stuff for work. And after he'd eaten, he'd fall asleep in front of the telly, usually with his mouth wide open.

But tonight he was shuffling about in his slippers making Mum a cup of tea. Mum couldn't crash out on the sofa, though, or even talk about her day. She was too busy wandering around admiring all the things Dad had done today.

'Boys, just look at these clean windows,' she called.

'OK, we're looking at them,' I said. 'Now what happens.'

Then Mum sat down in the kitchen saying how lovely it was to have a meal cooked for her for a change!

'Well, from now on, the kitchen is my domain, my little kingdom,' announced Dad. 'You are to leave everything to me, Jessica, all right?'

'You won't get any argument from me,' said Mum.

Then Dad brought in his vegetarian stew and handed round generous portions. 'Just tuck in,' he said. 'I've made enough for seconds.'

'Eeugh,' shouted Elliot, spraying his first mouthful right across the table.

'I should have brought an umbrella,' I quipped.

'Elliot, that is no way to behave at the table,' said Mum.

'But it's disgu—' he began.

'Not another word,' interrupted Mum fiercely.

'I don't think I got the flavour quite right,' said Dad.

'What flavour?' I murmured to Elliot. It didn't taste of anything except stale socks.

'Eat up, boys,' said Mum. 'It's wonderfully

filling.'

Elliot whispered to me, 'I'd rather eat my own bogies than any more of Dad's stew.'

'You know what,' I whispered back, 'I think I'd rather eat your bogies too.'

**7.15 p.m.**
'I'd sack Dad,' Elliot has just announced to me.

'After one day?'

'Yeah, he's rubbish. I knew he would be. Dads are just not meant to be mums.'

## Chapter Two
# Early-Morning Fire

**7.35 p.m.**
Spent a ton of time – a whole twenty minutes – trying to write my history essay. But now my arm is aching and so is my brain. And I had to stop for the sake of my health.

The trouble is, this essay is already late, you know. Even worse, my history teacher is also the deputy head, Mr Beach, known to all as Beachy Head. And he's scarier than Godzilla. Like today, when I gently explained to him why my history essay might be a tiny bit delayed, he immediately clenched his teeth like a ferocious bulldog and snapped, 'I want your essay in my hand first thing Tuesday morning and I very much hope, for your sake, that it's a good one.'

I'm not at all hopeful about it being good. Or even average. But it isn't really my fault, as I try my hardest to listen to his lessons. But there's something about Beachy Head's voice which sends my ears instantly to sleep.

On the bright side, I have managed to write twelve whole lines. On the not so bright side, that's actually my entire essay. Still, they always say, leave people wanting more. And maybe it's better than I think.

**7.40 p.m.**
No, I don't think so either.

**7.41 p.m.**
There's something you should know about me and school.

We don't get on.

I've never liked it, never fitted in. But I'm stuck there with teachers in my face all day long. And if you asked any of them about me, I know exactly what they'd say: 'Louis is ludicrously dim and extremely lazy.'

But I'm not – well, I'm not lazy anyway, because every single night I study for hours. Only it's a subject we never spend a second on at school – comedy.

And I'm as good at telling jokes, as I am rubbish at all my lessons.

So my dream, my one and only ambition, is to be a comedian. But first I have to be discovered. And for that you need an agent.

Well, I've got one.

Maddy goes to a different school to me. We met at a drama club, as she loves acting. But unfortunately she gets such a massive attack of nerves every time she steps onto a stage, she has had to give up on her dream of being a world-famous actress. And she has decided to become an agent instead.

I'm her very first client, and already she's helped me to appear on a television talent show called *Kids with Attitude*. It's on a satellite channel, so maybe you haven't seen it yet. But trust me, it's awesome.

Each week there are twelve contestants and viewers vote for their winner. They all go on to the Grand Final. The All Winners Show. And the winner of that will get their own half-hour Christmas show.

Well, I went on the show – telling jokes. I *so* wanted to win.

I came second. A parrot beat me. The shame of it, I know. I was like totally crushed until they decided one of the runners-up would also be allowed on the winners' show.

And they chose – me.

Any day now they are going to ring up with the date of the All Winners Show and then – well, Maddy is totally convinced I'll win outright this time. That means I'll also get my own Christmas show, and after that I just won't have time to go to school any more. I'll be far too busy travelling the world, making people laugh and generally leading the life of an international jet-setter.

**8.10 p.m.**
One more thing I should have told you about Maddy and me is that she's not only my agent and friend – she's also just become my girlfriend. We haven't actually been out on any dates yet. Well, you've got to build up to that, haven't you?

But I think it's time I got cracking on that.

**8.25 p.m.**
Just rang Maddy. Right away she said excitedly, '*Kids with Attitude* haven't …?'

'No, not yet, but I called you, Maddy, to find out when you'd like to meet up for our' – I lowered my voice here without quite knowing why – 'first date?'

Immediately she sounded a bit flustered. 'Well, er, when do you think?'

'I've cleared my diary for you,' I said. (Heard someone say that on a TV show once and thought it had sounded pretty cool.) 'So you just name the time and place and I will be there. In person.' I was sounding dead relaxed, but actually I had this odd sort of beating in my heart.

'What about Friday evening?' she suggested.

'It is in my diary already. Would you like to go to Luigi's?'

'Only if we go halves, as it's very expensive.'

'Money is never a problem, Maddy, when I ask a girl out.' How suave was that? And just to make it really clear, I added, 'So I'm paying for you too.'

After I put the phone down, my heart was still beating weirdly fast. This really is it.

## Tuesday November 19th

**7.25 a.m.**

Woken up by Elliot charging into my room, yelling, 'Fire! Fire! Isn't it brilliant?'

'What are you talking about?' I began. Then I heard the smoke alarms doing their stuff downstairs and sprang out of bed.

A bleary-eyed Mum joined us on the landing. 'What's happening, and where's your dad?'

At that moment Dad dashed out of the kitchen.

'Hey, everyone,' he called up to us. 'Sorry for disturbing your sleep. But there's absolutely nothing to worry about.'

'Why have the smoke alarms gone off, then?' asked Elliot.

'Just a tiny little accident. I thought I'd surprise you with warm croissants for breakfast, but I put them in the toaster ...'

'Oh, Dad,' began Elliot.

'It was a lovely thought,' trilled Mum as smoke started billowing up the stairs, 'and no harm done.'

After Dad had sped into the kitchen again, Elliot muttered, 'I hate croissants and—'

'Don't say that,' interrupted Mum. 'This can't be easy for your dad.'

'Not easy for us either,' said Elliot, 'having to eat all his food.' Elliot stomped downstairs again and then called, 'Mum, we've run out of milk.'

'Not your mum's problem!' shouted Dad. 'And I'm on to it,' he added as he tore out of the house.


**9.00 a.m.**
Beachy Head moves like a panther. I don't mean he walks around on all fours (I'd love to see him doing that), but you don't even realise he's nearby until you feel his hot breath right on

your neck.

I'd only arrived at school for a millionth of a second when I got a full blast of hot air. I whirled round. There was Beachy Head, glaring down at me.

'I hope you have your essay with you,' he growled.

I dug about in my bag and brought out my history exercise book. 'It's all in there,' I said, and to lighten the atmosphere I added, 'Enjoy.'

Not a flicker of a smile back. He just glided soundlessly away with my exercise book tucked under his arm.

**9.05 a.m.**
Do you know what I wish? That we still did colouring-in, at school. I was incredibly good at that. But I guess I peaked too early, as now I'm solidly rubbish at everything. Still, you never have to worry being bottom of the class when I'm around.

**3.20 p.m.**
It was the last lesson of the day – double maths – when the school secretary bustled in. She thinks she's so important and struts about with a permanent smell under her nose. Anyway, she whispered something to the teacher. I was

hoping she was saying the drains had packed up and we all had to go home for a month.

But instead the teacher announced that Beachy Head (only he didn't call him that, of course) wanted to see me immediately. I left to whispers of, 'Oooh, who's in big trouble?'

Beachy Head had obviously read my history essay. (Well, it wouldn't take him very long, would it?) But why couldn't he just have written something rude at the bottom of it like a normal teacher? Why did he have to go to all the bother of seeing me?

The secretary escorted me to Beachy Head's lair, and then walked briskly away. I knocked on his door. I didn't hear anything. But he was pretty ancient and probably a bit deaf, so I knocked again, more loudly, and then I gave several raps all together. He must have heard that.

He did. The door burst open so violently it nearly flew off its hinges. And he stood there, breathing fire at me. 'What on earth do you think you are doing?'

Talk about daft questions, but I explained ever so patiently, 'I'm knocking on your door, as you said you wanted to see me – but I can go away again if you've changed your mind,' I added eagerly. 'And I won't be offended at all.'

'I will tell you when I wish to see you,' said

Beachy Head. But he just had, hadn't he? 'For now, you will station yourself outside my room and wait there until I decide to send for you.'

So I'm being told off for going to see him – when he'd just told me to go and see him. I tell you, all adults are completely bonkers.

**3.35 p.m.**
The school bell has rung. It's the end of school, so by rights I could just go home. This is my time now.

**3.45 p.m.**
Yeah, I'm still hanging about outside Beachy Head's room. I really, really hate waiting around like this. So to cheer us all up, here's a joke. An educational one, as well.

*In ancient times, when a knight was killed in battle, what sign did they put on his grave?*
*Rust in Peace.*

I really love that one. Would you like another one? Sorry, no time, as Beachy Head has just shouted through the door, 'You may come in now.'

Got a horrible feeling I'm not going to enjoy what happens next.

# LOUIS THE LAUGH RETURNS!
## The brilliantly funny sequel to
## My Parents Are Driving Me Crazy

ISBN 978-1-78270-172-9

What can you do when you're trapped
in a TECHNOLOGY TIME WARP?
My parents have decided my brother Elliot
and I spend too much time 'glued to screens'
and now they've come up with their worst
idea EVER – a TOTAL BAN on all tablets,
computers and mobiles! I need a plan to
FIGHT BACK against their 'digital detox',
and FAST! Can my best friend Maddy
come to the RESCUE?

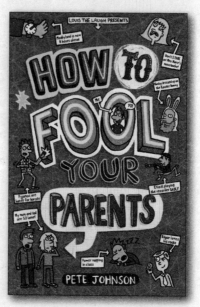